SOW

TIM CURRAN

ISBN 978-1-63789-622-8
Macabre Ink is an imprint of Crossroad Press Publishing

For information address Crossroad Press at 141 Brayden Dr., Hertford, NC 27944
www.crossroadpress.com

Cover art and design by David Dodd

First Crossroad Press Edition

1

Later on, Richard decided it was during the second trimester that his wife stopped being pregnant and started being possessed.

Maybe the fifteenth or sixteenth week is when it really became noticeable. That's when Molly ceased being a mother with child and became a host for something else entirely. She had been acting strange for some time, strange even for a first-time mother; then one night he had woken next to her, feeling a torpid heat rolling off her and smelling a sharp, almost chemical odor that clung to her like sweat. There in the dead of a warm August night, a perfectly ordinary night, he became convinced that what was lying at his side was not a woman, but a bloated and living pestilence.

2

But who could he turn to with that revelation?

Other fathers he knew admitted they found their wives somewhat unsightly while they were expecting, growing larger and less feminine by the day, but what Richard was experiencing was light years beyond that. Sleeping next to Holly in the darkness, occupying the same space with her, filled him with a loathing beyond anything he had ever known before. An atavistic revulsion like plunging his hand into the maggot-swollen belly of a dead cat.

He could barely even admit it to himself.

The sight of her reminded him of spiders and crawling things, worms and mating insects. Malignant things that sucked blood and webbed up their prey. And worse than that, maybe, was the idea that what was growing inside her was not a fetus, but a parasite.

Christ, what's wrong with you? How can you be thinking such awful things?

But he did not know. He only knew he could not stop thinking them.

Day by day then, he could only watch the terrible change coming over her, watch her belly expand as that nameless thing in her grew fat and fleshy, leeching her of nutrients and sucking away her mind. He lost himself in the murky vacuum of denial, playing the happy, proud papa…even though his stomach was weak and his skin was literally crawling.

He told himself it was all his imagination.

In the morning, he'd wake with a positive attitude, more than ready to cast off all those wild and ugly thoughts that filled his mind, but one look at Holly and it all came back. There was no earthly doubt in his mind—what was inside her was not remotely human.

She had, in effect, been invaded.

3

No one else saw it, of course.

Her friends and his friends, family members...they all came to see the expectant mother, bearing gifts and good wishes. The men talked of their firstborn and the women talked of labor. They were all happy and content and so was Holly. Until they left, that was. Then the change would come over her.

She would lie in bed, propped up by pillows, ringing her damn bell and like a salivating dog, Richard would come running, hoping beyond hope that his smiling, cheerful wife would not leave again. That that other...*creature* would not return. But it always did. The sallow-faced woman with the crooked grin and the shining eyes like bits of broken glass. It got so he began to tremble and perspire just reaching for the doorknob to their (her) room, which he began to acquaint with the latch of a coffin.

After Holly's Uncle Dick and Aunt Pauline left one Saturday afternoon, the bell began to ring immediately. Richard poured a shot of bourbon down his throat and went up the stairs like he was carrying a sack of bricks on his back. Outside the door, he hesitated, his guts crawling up the back of his throat. He reached for the door...but he couldn't bring himself to touch it. It was like reaching out to throw open the door of a mausoleum.

Then behind the door, that rasping treble: "Well? I'm waiting, Richard. Don't play possum…I can *smell* you out there."

He grasped the knob and threw the door open. He tried to put a smile on his face, but the best he could do was something just this side of a grimace. It was hot in the room, not just warm but *torrid*, sweltering, steaming and rank like a miasmic swamp. In his mind, he was seeing pale green vapors seething from her oily skin. And the smell…things pulled up from bogs and stagnant ponds.

How? he wondered. *How could the change come so quickly?*

When Uncle Dick and Aunt Pauline had been in the room, she had looked pink-cheeked, glowing, and effusive with life. The perfect little happy mother, beautiful, radiating with that warm inner glow. There had been no bad odors. Just a slight memory of lilacs and hand lotion. But now?

"Don't hover there like a little worm, Richard," Holly said to him with a voice like a razor scraped over yellow bone.

But he did hover. He was dizzy and weak and almost overcome by what he smelled, felt, and saw. This was not his wife. Richard did not know who or what it was, but it certainly was not Holly. The thing sat there, staring at him with flat reptilian eyes, hair like brittle yellow straw, an obese and obscene creature fattened in a swill barrel, engorged like a sponge soaked in grease.

"Come here, Richard," she said.

She was not asking, she was demanding. He could not move. The sight of her and the aura that hung about her put his stomach into his throat. His breath would not come and his eyes began to water.

"Richard." Her fingers reached out to him like withered sticks snapped from a winter-dead bush, her eyes shiny like wet beetles. "*Come here, Richard.*"

He stumbled forward, trying to smile, clenching his teeth tightly. As he neared her, he became aware of a fishy odor she exuded, of the rancid heat billowing off her. It was like nearing a bubbling cauldron of tallow and bones: hot and sickening.

Holly flashed him a bloodless smile when he neared the bed. "I need something, Richard, and you are going to go and get it for me."

"What? What do you want?"

"A fetal Doppler," she said.

He knew what that was. An ultrasound Doppler that could detect high-frequency sound waves reflected off the fetal heart. People used them to listen to their baby's heartbeat.

"You want to listen to…to the baby's heart?"

She kept smiling. "I want to hear what baby has to say."

Richard could not speak. He stood over her, trying to focus his eyes, trying to make sense of what she had just said. *I want to hear what baby has to say*. Like…well, *like* the baby was talking to her. But that was just insane.

Holly looked up at him with dull, gelid eyes. They were like depthless pools of formaldehyde. "You want that, too, don't you, Richard? Don't you want to know what our babies have to say?"

Babies. Is that what she said? He swallowed. "But the ultrasound…there's only one child."

She tittered. "*Was*, Richard, *was* one. It's been dividing, you see."

4

When he came back later with the Stork Radio Fetal Doppler unit, Holly was there. Not that horrid thing, but Holly. She lay in bed, reading from some dusty old book. Her eyes were bright and blue and lovely.

"Ah, a stranger bearing gifts," she said when she saw the package. "What have you brought me? If it's pastrami on rye, I'll love you forever."

"No...I...do you want me to get you a sandwich?"

"I'm just kidding, dummy." Holly narrowed her eyes. "Are you all right, Richard? You look...you don't look good at all."

He sat on the bed. "I'm fine, just tired. I brought you the Doppler you wanted."

"The what?"

"The Doppler," he said, pulling out a box from the bag.

"Am I forecasting the weather?"

Same old Holly. Quick, funny. Where was that other thing? Hiding under the bed? In the closet? Waiting up in the hot darkness of the attic, sucking the blood out of flies?

Richard showed Holly what he'd brought.

"Oh, that's great! I've always wanted one of those!"

"You asked me to get it for you."

"I did?"

He nodded. "You said…you said you wanted to hear what the baby had to say…"

Holly started laughing. "Oh, really? I said that?"

"You did."

She stopped laughing, put a hand to his forehead. "Are you feeling all right, Richard? You seem a little warm, a little…I don't know…confused."

He tried to tell her what she had said, but as always she had no memory of it. She just looked at him sympathetically like he was losing his mind. And maybe he was. He only wished he'd lose it completely already. This bouncing back between madness and sanity was killing him.

"Lay down beside me, Richard," Holly said. "You need a rest."

He didn't bother arguing further. He lay down next to her, losing himself in her scent, which was French vanilla and lilac. She smelled wonderful. She'd always smelled wonderful. At the edge of sleep, he opened his eyes, smelling something moldy and dusty. It was her book. It looked very old, one of those antique folios that were big and heavy enough to crush a rat. She was already asleep, so he pulled it gently from her fingers and set it on the nightstand.

But not before seeing the title: *Confessions of the Essex Witch.*

5

It meant nothing, of course, and he was so good at denial by that point he actually believed it. Regardless of what he had seen, he told himself that all was right with the world and he was imagining things. Hallucinations, some weird sort of delirium brought about by stress and anxiety. What he needed to do was to admit to himself that something was going on with his head and to get some help. Maybe it was chemical or metabolic or even inherited. Who could say? The idea of going to a therapist disgusted him. Like most men, he was too proud to admit he might need help. The couch was for weaklings and drama queens, not ordinary, healthy guys like him.

But he was beginning to think differently now.

If they can get this shit out of my head, I'll happily sit on their fucking lap and suck my thumb if that's what it takes.

And these were the thoughts that flittered through his mind as he drifted off. As usual, his dreams were awful affairs where he was chased through a section of town he had never seen before and could never escape from. Walls closing in. Streets turning back into themselves. Doors that opened into black, spiraling gulfs. Stairways that climbed up into emptiness. And always, at his back, some nameless, dragging thing, a black and horrendous shadow that puffed out great clouds of white vapor.

Just after three, he opened his eyes.

He could smell the book right away. In the dead of night, it did not smell simply dusty and old like it had before, now it stank like the rotting hide of an animal: musky and noisome. He had no idea where Holly had gotten such a thing, but he was going to get rid of it. That's all there was to it.

In the moonlight coming in through the window, he could see Holly's sleeping form next to him. Her breathing was phlegmy and rattling like that of a tubercular old man. Something had shifted in the room, something had changed. He lay there, peering into the darkness, rivers of sweat running down his face, pooling at his throat.

"Holly?" he said under his breath.

He reached out for her and touched her neck, immediately pulling his hand away with a muted cry. It was not the smooth, angular expanse of neck he knew so well but a greasy pelt of hoglike bristles.

It can't be happening again.

Holly reached out a hand to grasp his own and it was not feminine and long-fingered, but a hideous claw, black and wrinkled like a prune.

He knew then.

He knew what he was lying next to.

"Oh God," he muttered, his mouth thick with terror.

The air was hot and gummy like molasses and he could barely draw a breath. He turned his head slowly and she was sitting up, her eyes reflective like chips of quartz. She had something on her lap: the Doppler unit.

"What…what are you doing?" he said.

Her voice was ragged like well-chewed meat. "I'm listening."

"To what?"

"To what's inside me," she said, her breath sour and pungent. "I'm listening to the music of my womb."

Shaking and gagging, he stumbled from the room.

There was no earthly doubt of it: he was losing his mind.

6

He didn't sleep the rest of the night.

He dozed intermittently on the couch downstairs, sweating through myriad nightmares in which Holly gave birth to faceless monsters and slithering offspring. Things that crept into his lap and cuddled there like fetal jellyfish, wet and stinging.

He awoke each time shivering, hot and cold, his belly full of sharp, cutting blades. Finally, he gave it up, facing another day weary and worn and threadbare like an old throw rug that had seen too many feet and too many years. He pounded the dust out of himself and made a pot of coffee. Black, strong. After his second cup, he felt a little better. As good as he ever did these days. He hadn't eaten in some time, but the thought of food made him want to vomit. So he sat at the kitchen table, watching the sun come up over the treetops like a great burning eye, spilling color over roofs and lawns and quiet streets.

He drank his coffee and smoked a cigarette, knowing he had quit years ago but with no memory of starting again. All the while, his mind blazed with tapestries of madness, seamless and finely knit, vibrant in their chromatic lunacy. He thought of Dr. Frazer, Holly's ob-gyn, and what she would say if he admitted to her what was happening to his wife. Then he thought of an exorcist. Finally, he thought of committing her, but knowing the only one who would be committed was himself.

Time passed and the coffeepot emptied and the ashtray overflowed, but through it all, there were no answers. Richard approached it from every angle, looked in every nook and cranny of his mind and in every possible crevice of reality, but there was no solution. Nothing that made sense. Nothing rational that would explain it all. There was nothing to do but smoke and chew his nails and quietly go mad. What was happening was not to be found in the real world. The explanation could only be found in superstition, located in dark closets and darker cellars, places where the light of reason did not shine. This is where Richard would have to put his hands if he wished to find answers. For only in these places, the unlit caverns of the mind, would he be able to grasp slimy and insane truths and hold them up to be studied and gasped over.

About ten, the bell rang.

And with it came the secret dread and mystical pain Richard knew so well. The bell kept ringing, tinny and shrill, summoning him. His hands shook and his neck went hot with sweat and his guts literally ached like a heroin addict going cold off the needle. Something inside him was wound so tightly he thought it might tear open from sheer internal stress and when that happened, he would himself unwind into an untidy heap of knotted string and tangled wires.

The bell.

Summoning him.

Calling him.

He butted his cigarette, decided that going crazy was simply not an option.

He would have to look this in the face, whatever it was, identify it and only then could he hope to crush it.

At the bottom of the stairs, he paused.

He did not smell the badness.

Did not feel it.

At the top, he paused again. Still, he did not sense anything up there but his wife.

He thought: *It's just Holly right now. Don't let her see what's in your eyes, don't let her suspect what's in your mind. She's ignorant of it all and the truth would shatter her just as it's shattering you. Don't give the game away.*

And behind the door?

Just Holly, sitting there with pillows stacked up behind her. Her arms were folded and her blue eyes were narrowed. "Some nurse you are, Richard. Dr. Frazer tells me to stay in bed, so I stay in bed. She tells you to look after me and you're nowhere to be found. Baby and I are half starving to death and where are you?"

Richard tried to smile, never realizing until of late how much effort went into that simple flex of facial muscles. "Sorry, honey. I was drinking my coffee and listening to the radio."

She sniffed the air. "And smoking? Oh, Richard, you're not smoking again, are you?"

"Guilty as charged."

"Well, do it outside then." She looked at him, seeing something, but unsure. "I'm starting to wonder if you're the one who should be in bed. If you don't mind me saying so, you look like shit."

"Again, guilty. Not sleeping right."

"Hmm. Well, fetch my breakfast, then you can nap." Holly began counting off on her fingers. "I want two pieces of toast with jelly, Corn Flakes, and a cup of my herbal tea. Yes, that'll do...wait, how about a couple scrambled eggs, too?"

"You got it."

Maybe there is something wrong with me, he thought. *She seems completely normal.*

"And Richard? Be a love and open that window...it smells funny in here."

He did everything she asked, happily so. Seeing her like that filled him with hope and calmed his nerves. Jesus, maybe he had some kind of fever going. Maybe he had better quit with the caffeine and nicotine and make with three squares a day and some sleep. He made her food, whistling all the while, putting the dishes and silverware on an antique platter she had picked up at a yard sale. When he went back into her room, she was reading that witch book again and the air in there was hot, stale, and unpleasant.

"Holly?" he said, already knowing.

She looked up at him, eyes gleaming like dirty nickels. "It's about time, Richard. It's about high fucking time."

The hag was back.

She stared holes through him, made him bleed inside. He could barely hold up the tray, the metallic eyes of the Holly-thing drilling through him, getting down into his guts and poisoning his soul. He tried to pull in a breath, but the air was grainy and dusty, his lungs full of soap flakes. Holly did not blink and she did not move...a sightless and lewd thing painted on the accordion board of a freak house, gazing out with pickled eyes and smiling with gnashing yellow teeth.

"Bring my food," she said finally. "And close that damn window before I freeze to death."

Richard, his belly filled with curdled cream, walked over to the bed and set the tray down before his wife. Like an automaton, he stumbled over to the window and shut it...then, something unfolding in him, something pissed-off, he took hold of the sash and threw the window up all the way.

"I said—"

"I heard what you said," he told her, turning and meeting her gaze with one of his own. "I just don't agree with it."

Her reaction was instantaneous.

He had known Holly for eight years. What was sitting on the bed was not Holly. Her face was like a pallid moon ringed by a corona of dead straw that might have been called hair. Her eye sockets were swollen red and the eyes themselves a dirty and tarnished silver. Her mouth was pulled into a contorted snarl.

Richard almost fell over.

And then he did when the window he had just opened came slamming down, hairline cracks threading through the glass. A vase with dried flowers on the bureau shattered, chips of green glass raining over the carpet.

Holly shrieked: "You are not the one who will make the decisions! You are not the one who will tell me what is and what is not! I will be the one that does the telling! I will do the telling and the calling and sowing! Do you understand, you little fucking worm? And what I can call and what I can sow are that which you will not want to know of!"

Richard had pulled himself up, leaning against the wall for support. "Where's my wife? What have you done with my wife?"

"It is not what we have *done* with your little wifey, but what we'll *do* with her." She began to laugh and the tray of food he had brought went sailing through the air and slammed into the wall, tea and eggs and cereal running down the paneling in a wet and globby mess. Richard could not say he saw her throw it. It may have thrown itself. "Now bring me some food, the food I like. I want *meat,* Richard. Not cooked or smoked, but raw and juicy and well-marbled. Do not drain the blood from it. I wish to taste the saltiness of the meat and sip the red juices.

Do you understand me? Do you understand what our babies need?"

Richard stumbled to the door, whatever strength he'd found evaporated now like a puddle. "Please—"

"Shut up! Do not crawl and cower, you make me fucking ill!" Holly said. "And Richard? Know this and know this well. No more defiance or what you dream of will be given flesh and what coils in your lap will call you by name." She cackled then, the sound of glass crunched underfoot and knife blades drawn across rusty iron. "Don't piss us off, Richard."

7

"I think I'm losing my mind," Richard said a few days later.

Maitland sipped his beer. "Buddy, you lost that years ago."

"I'm serious, Mike. I've never been more serious in my life."

Maitland saw that he was and choked off any smart-ass comments he was thinking of making. Richard looked like hell. He was losing weight, dark crescents set beneath each eye. His hands were shaking and there was a look about him that was, well, *frightening*. Like an accident victim about to go into shock.

"Tell me," Maitland said.

Richard just looked at him and maybe *through* him at something on the other side that was scaring the shit out of him. "It's Holly. It's trouble with Holly."

"Not the baby—"

Richard shook his head, pulling off his beer. "Not in the way you'd think. I'd even welcome something like that. At least, at least it would be normal."

"Maybe you better just tell me."

They'd been friends for years. They'd bowled in the same league, played slow-pitch together. Drank a lot of beer and had a lot of talks. Richard had been the best man at Maitland's second wedding, even though that had only lasted a few months like most of his relationships. Richard couldn't think of anyone in the world he trusted as much as Maitland, yet the idea of saying any of this, of actually putting it into words, was almost more than he could take.

"C'mon, Richard. You can tell me anything."

"Can I?"

"Yes." He meant it.

"Okay...okay, here goes. Molly's been, well, not herself lately. And I don't mean she's been moody or even a little bitchy like pregnant women get, I mean she's been someone else entirely. In fact, I think she's possessed."

Maitland sat there, waiting for the inevitable punch line. "You mean...*what?* By like a demon or a spirit or something?"

"Yes. Or something."

"C'mon, Richard, this isn't funny."

"No, it sure as hell isn't."

So he let it all fly. He opened his mouth and he couldn't seem to clamp it shut once the words and madness started to pour out like floodwaters overflowing a levee. He nearly drowned Maitland before he was done. But he got it out. Holly's other personality, her demands for raw meat and blood, the apparent instances of telekinesis and possibly even telepathy, the idea that their baby had *divided* like an amoeba. Every weird and unlikely and downright impossible thing he'd witnessed in the past three or four weeks.

"I bought her this fetal Doppler, Mike. It's one of those things you can listen to the baby's heartbeat with...only I think she's using it for something else."

Maitland finished his beer. Even so, his throat was dry. "Like what...what else could she use it for?"

Richard grinned over his stein. "She...she *listens* to what the babies are saying. I heard her the other night. She was talking to someone in there. I stood outside the door, listening, but it was all muffled. I couldn't hear, so I…I cracked the door a bit and she had that Doppler probe on her belly and she was sitting there, Mike, sitting on the bed…her eyes all silver and gleaming, this terrible grin on her face. She was nodding and nodding, saying shit like, *'Yes, yes, yes, I can hear you, my angels, I can hear what my babies say. There will come a time and a place, yes, and then we'll have what was promised. Oh yes, my angels, we will have the blood and the meat of all the sons and the daughters, all those little bones will be ours to covet…we will not be denied our birthright, we will not be denied soft pink throats…'* That's what she was saying, Mike. That's what I heard her say, like she was just repeating what was being *told* to her.

"I…I was scared, Mike. I've never been so completely scared in my life. And that voice she was speaking with, it wasn't her voice…it was an old voice, raw and grating like that of some hag." Richard pulled down his beer, studied the emptiness of his mug like maybe he was looking into himself. "Then…Holly fell silent and she turned and looked at me…and those eyes, Jesus, Mike, I've never seen eyes like that before. So empty, so dead, so soulless. Puppet eyes. And she said, *'Oh yes, yes, my babies, you're right, the little worm is listening to us, snooping on us. You'll not bear witness against us, Richard, because no one would ever believe you. The time is coming and soon when those of true faith will be called upon.'*"

"That's enough, Richard," Maitland said. He looked angry. He looked like he wanted nothing better than to slap Richard right across the face and maybe keep slapping him. "I've heard enough. Now, I want you to take a breather. I want you to sit there and think about what you just told me and then I want you tell me if this is the truth. Because if you're messing with me, I'm going to come right over that table and kick your ass so hard your mama's gonna roll over in her grave and say ouch.

And if you're telling the truth…then, well, you're scaring the living shit right out of me."

It didn't take Richard long. "I'm telling the truth."

Maitland just nodded. He motioned the waitress over and ordered two more beers and two shots of Jack Daniel's. When they came, Richard and he drank in silence.

"All right," Maitland said. "I don't know what to tell you. How about her doctor? That might be a place to start."

"She refuses to see her doctor, to see any doctor. She doesn't even want any more ultrasounds."

"Okay, there is one thing you could do. But it's kind of ugly."

"What?"

"Commit her. Have a psych come in and see her. He sees any of what you've been seeing, he'll draw up the papers and all you'll have to do is sign them."

Richard shook his head. "Won't do any good. Around other people she's just Holly. I'm the one who'd be committed."

"What about medical care?"

"She has a midwife. Mrs. Crouch."

Richard explained that he had only heard the name a few days before himself. Apparently, this mysterious Mrs. Crouch only came by whenever he was out. "Holly said…the *other* Holly said that Mrs. Crouch takes care of her and I can go back to work, I'm not needed or wanted. She's also the one, Holly claims, that brought her that book on witches."

Maitland just nodded. "I don't know what in the hell to even tell you. I wish there was something I could do."

"There is."

Richard said he was going back to the office tomorrow. That Holly would be alone and that was he was betting this Mrs. Crouch would show when he was gone.

"And you want me to be there when she does?"

"No, I want you to be parked down the street. I want you to get her license number, something. I want you to find out who this woman is. Please, Mike, I need you to do this. You follow people for a living. It's what you do."

"C'mon, quit the cloak and dagger, I'm just an insurance investigator, I'm not a cop."

"No, but you know how to get the dirt on people, don't you? And plenty of your friends are cops."

Maitland shrugged. "I guess I could happen to be in the neighborhood."

Richard smiled.

8

Richard left before Holly was up the next day.

He didn't have the courage to go up and see her when he got home from his meeting with Maitland, but he had a real nasty feeling that she knew all about it. It seemed there was very little she *didn't* know about. So he stayed downstairs where he'd pretty much been living anyway. Holly, the real Holly, had not been back in days now. It was just that hag living up in their bedroom, plotting with what was growing in her belly that Richard was certain was not even human.

When he was safely ensconced in his office, he got on the Internet and researched the Essex Witch. There was no shortage of information. The Essex Witch, real name Alizon Clove, was hanged in the English county of Essex for the crime of witchcraft in 1583. She was supposedly responsible for the hexing murders of a dozen people in and around a place called the Grey Hop Forest. According to her own confession, given apparently without undue coercion, she claimed that she had sold her soul to a pagan devil or familiar spirit named Old Jack Hobb on her thirteenth birthday, been "nigh compeled to," as had all the women in her family going back to "antient times." In exchange, she was taught the "olde ways" and the "proven pathe," given the power of "blight and pox" with which she could kill or cripple any that she chose.

Alizon Clove was nearly eighty when she was arrested and brought to trial. She had a dire history behind her of witching and was greatly feared in the Grey Hop Forest region. What brought it all to a head was the accusation of fourteen-year-old Jane Penden, the daughter of a local merchant, that Alizon Clove had "bewitched and enticed" her, offering her great rewards "of the fleshe and the soule" if she were to give herself willingly and bodily during the Sabbat to the devil Old Jack Hobb. Alizon Clove told the girl that she would carry Hobb's children, which would be "of greate and peculiar likenesse to their father" and then, upon birth, hand them over to the old witch. Whereupon, she would be granted "any and all favors due unto her." Jane Penden had been chosen for this because she was a virgin and pure of heart and unblemished of soul.

According to court transcripts:

> *The said examinate Jane Penden sayth, that nigh two years ago, the old woman of the Grey Hop wood, (called Alizon Clove, alias Widow Crouch) did sundry times advise the examinate to give herself bodily to a devil here known as Old Jack Hobb so that he would have knowledge of her and seek coitus wherein she would bear his seed. Hence and beforehand, sayth Alizon Clove, a familiar or imp would appear to her of the name Pigwicken; and that she, this examinate, would let him suck at some part of her; and she might have and do what she would. And so not long after these perswasions, to this examinate there appeared unto her a thing like unto a pygmy hog*

> *or hideous hobgoblin: speaking unto her, this examinate, and desiring her to give him her soule, and he would give her power to do any thing she would: whereupon this examinate being therewithall inticed, the said Pigwicken did with his mouth (this examinate sayth) sucke at her breast, a little below her paps; the imp knowing hunger of blood and milke; said breast which place did remaine blew halfe a yeare next after: which said Pigwicken hence did appeare to this examinate regularly and of at night in preparedness for said intercourse of the devil Jack Hobb.*

This scant evidence was enough to lead to the arrest of Alizon Clove and her imprisonment in the local gaol. When her hut was searched, the magistrates discovered a number of "claye and haire dolls" with which it was claimed that she had not only witched the locals, but brought about disease and death. There were further accusations concerning grave robbery and ghoulism, divination and child murder. Interestingly enough, the courts were at a loss as to what to do with Alizon Clove. Showing uncharacteristic leniency and insight, she was neither tortured nor sentenced to death. The evidence of the witch dolls in her hut were incontrovertible, given the laws of the time. But other than that, there was only local gossip and rumor and the word of Jane Penden. The "murders" were actually suicides, each of the victims having hanged themselves. Some twelve such suicides in a matter of months would seem statistically improbable, but the courts did not think even these constituted due cause to execute the old woman. Given time and public pressure, Clove would have certainly gone to the gallows, but fate interceded.

Alizon Clove freely confessed.

Her confession ran some eighty pages and was recorded by court officials. According to what Richard found on the Internet, the witch's confession was quite lively and damning. She admitted to hexing all twelve of the suicides, forcing them to take their own lives by application of the "wicked eye" and the "counting noose." She also admitted to robbing graves for the raw materials of her craft, to extorting local farmers with sorcery, to calling up the spirits of the dead and certain "discarnate soulls" to do her bidding. She said that Old Jack Hobb was a forest devil that had been known to her family "since olden tymes." She admitted practicing the black mass, ritual sacrifice, and of holding the Witches' Sabbat on nights of the new moon. What she would not do is implicate any of her fellow witches, name her familiars, or confirm any of what Jane Penden had testified to. But other than that, she spoke at great length of her guilt and seemed to the court to be "neare anxious" to go to the gallows.

And in 1584 she did just that.

And so ended the legend and times of Alizon Clove.

Richard spent nearly three hours reading through court documents and summaries that had been uploaded to the Web. Interesting stuff. But it didn't give him any answers. What could something over 400 years old have to do with Holly today? And that was all in England, not here in America.

Of course, as far as he was concerned, the most damning bit of evidence was Alizon Clove herself. She was also known as "Widow Crouch," "Dark Alizon," and "Missy Crouch" to her witch brethren. This Jane Penden confirmed.

Missy Crouch, witch.

Mrs. Crouch, midwife.

Then he knew.

9

When he saw it, he nearly screamed.

It was that horrific.

Just the sight of the *thing* generated such feelings of despair and horror that he was nearly overwhelmed. He stood there in the doorway to that awful dank catacomb he had once shared with his wife and swooned.

Holly was awake, except, of course, it was not Holly.

It was never Holly anymore. Just that demented hag with the blackening teeth and the dripping quicksilver eyes that would burn a hole right through you if you stared into them long enough. No, not Holly. Something slimy and invertebrate, a lolling white obscenity like a human slug, horridly round and glistening as if it was sweating petroleum jelly.

"What…what is that?" Richard finally said.

"A teddy bear." Holly grinned, lips shriveling away from puckered and discolored gums that were speckled like a dog's tongue. "It's something for our babies, Richard. Of a likeness unto them. Blood calls to blood as a brother knows a brother."

Richard was speechless.

There was no doubt that his own wife, or what she had become, filled him with an almost primal disgust these days.

But this toy, this perversion of a teddy bear…it was hard to truly say what it was meant to represent. Surely not a bear or any earthly mammal. When he saw it sitting there on the nightstand, he thought some horrible little pygmy had crawled into the room. It was maybe twelve or fourteen inches high, legs crossed and three-fingered hands nested at its pendulous belly, looking, if anything, like a cross between a toad and a particularly degenerate-looking piglet with a scaly, ratlike tail. It had reticulated and beaded flesh covered in patchy, irregular tufts of greasy gray fur that looked bristled. From its broad, almost simian head there hung a plaited net of grayish hair that tangled down to its sloping shoulders and over its stark, anemic face in oily strands.

"It's…awful," he said, without even meaning to do so.

And it was, dear God, but it was.

Its skin was oddly flabby and loose, hanging in folds and pockets. And that face…like some starved and wizened baboon, wrinkled and aged, its pushed-in snout grinning with a mouthful of interlocked yellow teeth that were narrow as pegs and looked disturbingly sharp. Richard could imagine that mouth and those teeth tearing great bloody chunks out of you while the black eyes looked on with a deadly, sterile fascination.

"Why, it's merely a harmless toy," the hag said.

This was not a fucking toy.

This was not a teddy bear.

This was like some monstrous hybrid between a deranged, mutant ape and an African fetish doll. It was meant to inspire fear and loathing. He could see little cameos of himself reflected in its eyes as he approached it, feeling something unwind in his belly.

"It has a name, Richard…would you like to know it?"

He shook his head. No, he did not want to know that. Names implied personality and personality implied a soul and this thing could have neither. It was corrupt and profane.

Pigwicken.

Its name is Pigwicken.

Say its name, Richard. Say it aloud.

The words were said in his mind. The hag never opened her mouth. With the words came dominance and he could not refuse. "Pigwicken," he said, the very name on his tongue sickening him. "*Pigwicken.*"

The thing moved…shuddered, only momentarily, but Richard saw it. And not only did it shudder but it made a sound quite like a low squealing.

Dear God, it's fucking alive…that little horror is actually alive.

The hag grinned at him, enjoying his discomfort a little too much.

This was the familiar that Alizon Clove called up for Jane Penden. The filthy thing was here. Now. Four hundred years later.

It took everything he had not to knock that smirk off the hag's face. And she saw it, too. She saw what burned in him and she actually flinched, looking uncertain as if maybe she had gone too far, pushed him past the point of no return.

"Where did you get it?" he said. "Where did you get that ugly fucking horror?"

Holly sneered at him, drool glistening at her mouth. "Does it frighten you, Richard? Do you worry what it might be and what it might do? That, maybe, one dark night, you might find it cuddled up in bed with you?"

And that was exactly what worried him.

He had thought that very thing and Holly had liberated it from his mind. A game. It was all a game, he realized. For a moment there he'd been caught somewhere between pissing his pants out of sheer terror and jumping on the hag, wrapping his hands around her throat and squeezing until all the black shit came squirting out of her ears.

He thought: *Playing you, Richard. It's all about playing you. Knocking you down to some infantile, subservient level where you will do what you are told and you will not dare question this monstrosity that is possessing your wife. It's all about dominance.*

Remember that.

"You plan on keeping that heap of shit in my house?"

The hag smiled, her rotting teeth on full display. "Yes, I do, and there's not a damn thing you can do about it. Not if you value the life of your little wifey."

Richard took a step closer to the bed, got in so close to the hag that he could smell the rifled graves on her breath. "You're weak. You're frightened," he said. "Without her and without me, you're nothing and you know it."

"My babies are getting angry, Richard," the hag told him. "Every time you make them angry, they make your sweet little Holly suffer for it. Each time you disobey, they bite her...*from inside*."

He backed away because he realized that he honestly had no choice. Holly would be kept alive at least until the babies were born. Or until *whatever* was in her was born. Until then, the hag needed them both. But after that? After that?

Richard figured he knew what would come after that.

At the doorway, he stopped and turned. "I don't pretend to know what you're up to and I'll probably never know...or want to. But, understand this, you crazy fucking bitch. As my wife suffers, so will you. If you hurt her, nothing in heaven or hell will save you...or your crawling brood."

The hag just stared at him, eyes full of acid.

"One of these days, we're going to have a talk," he said. "All about some fucked-up inbred witch named Alizon Clove. And how she came to an end and how she's going to come to an end again."

10

Later, he wondered if there had been any real point to his bravado.

For honestly, he was scared.

Scared of the hag and scared of what was inside Holly. He was scared of a lot of things. And he was willing to bet the hag knew it. That she was feeding off it as her kind probably always did. But as scared as he was, he meant what he'd said. If that bitch hurt Holly, then she was going to suffer.

For hours after that little exchange, he sat in his easy chair downstairs, smoking and thinking, feeling roughly like a rat running the maze and fearing there really was no way out of this Medieval bullshit. Jesus, he was thirty-five years old, an account rep for a veneer and siding firm. He lived in an ordinary Wisconsin town in a terribly run-of-the-mill and conservative neighborhood. He bowled. He liked the Green Bay Packers and takeout pizza. He collected football cards from the 1950s and '60s. The most exciting thing that had ever happened to him was when he won $1,500 on a scratch-off ticket. He was so terribly boring and terribly average, he routinely made census-takers yawn. The bottom line here was that he had no business dealing with witches and possession and evil imps from hell.

He simply had no business in any of this.

They had picked the wrong guy here. He didn't even like horror movies, let alone living in one.

Thinking these things and knowing what was upstairs, he tried to put it into perspective. Any sort of perspective. Even one that was lopsided as all hell. What was he really looking at here? What was he really thinking this was about?

Alizon Clove, a voice in his head told him. *That's what you think this is about. Some crazy old witch from across the pond that's been dead over four centuries. Somehow, some way, through some totally fucked-up and convoluted sense of logic, she has taken possession of your wife. And she has done so because she plans on doing what she set out to do back in the sixteenth century: bring to term the offspring of Old Jack Hobb. But instead of seeding Jane Penden, she has seeded Holly.*

Of course, that's exactly what he was thinking. To the letter. He hadn't wanted to admit it to himself, but it had been gathering wool in his head ever since he read all the historical accounts of the Essex Witch. So there it was, laid out before him. Now what? He sat there, smoking and waiting for the laughter to come. Because it was really ridiculous, wasn't it? Shit, it was the sort of thinking they committed people for.

Ten minutes later, the laughter still had not come.

As much as he hated the idea, he did *believe* it. And he had reached the point now where he could not possibly talk himself out of it. Maybe it was all the crap he'd been through. Maybe it had softened the soil of his mind so that just about anything would take root now.

You can fight against this, Richard, that voice said to him, *but in the end, you'll only be hurting yourself. Self-denial will only make this all harder. If you accept it, maybe you can bring this to an end.*

Sure, sure. And maybe believing bullshit like that would drive him just a little crazier than he already was. He tried approaching it one last time from the seat of reason. Maybe Holly wasn't possessed. Maybe she was just crazy...but that could not explain the telekinesis, those revolting odors, the physical changes she was suffering. Holly was someone or something else. She didn't seem capable of even pretending anymore.

That was it then.

The only explanation was a supernatural one, or at least the sort of phenomena you would call *supernatural*. That's where Richard was. He felt the last shreds of doubt fading from him, felt the cloying darkness of total superstitious belief. It was not a good feeling. It made him feel depressed and bleak and just utterly hopeless. But even so, he was not willing to throw reason and sanity completely to the wind. There was still a candle burning in his mind and its light was logic. Regardless of how deranged this all was, Richard was foolish enough to believe that even things like demonic possession had to follow some thread of logic. He just couldn't believe Holly had been selected at random.

But, dammit, there just wasn't a connection.

Richard's people were all Dutch and Scandinavian. Holly's were French and German. There was no connection to England or Essex that he knew of. Yet, there *had* to be. Somehow, there was a system at work here, a system with rules same as any other. He might not see it, but in his heart he knew it was there.

It had been quiet upstairs for some time now.

Not so much as a creak of the bed.

Maybe it was time for an acid test before he threw reason completely away.

He finished his cigarette and crept quietly up the stairs. The sun had not set all the way yet, but the light was fading fast. At the top of the stairs, he heard the wind pick up outside and rattle a few loose roofing tiles. The elm in the back yard creaked like a rusty hinge.

Silence.

Holly was not talking to "baby" or to herself for that matter. Richard wondered if maybe she was listening for him, playing one of her little games. And his rational self told him to call Dr. Frazer and drag her over here right now so she could see what Holly had become.

Richard moved soundlessly up the hallway. He stopped before the door and listened. And right away it came over him, that nameless terror. It oozed from his pores like sour sweat.

He put his hand on the doorknob and turned it very gently, opening the door a few inches. Holly was lying facedown, her breathing ragged but deep. She was sleeping. It stank in there as it always stank these days and there was a weird, subtle charge in the air like the aftermath of violence. He waited for the hag to roll over and offer him her toothy, demented grin.

But she did not move.

Pigwicken was there, of course. Sitting on the nightstand, staring at him, its grin huge and lunatic like that of some morbid ape. He wanted to smash it. To knock it to the floor and stomp the stuffing out of it...only he was afraid of what might run out.

There was something innately perverse about it, something that got down into his guts and scratched inside his skull. Maybe the way it stared or the way it grinned or maybe just the menace that bled from it like poison. It inspired a bone-deep revulsion like an especially large and bloated spider. What made it worse is that he knew what it was. Not a stuffed toy, but an imp, a familiar, and probably the source of the hag's power.

He got up close to it.

His heart was hammering, his nerve endings jangling. There wasn't enough spit to wet his mouth. It kept looking at him with those huge and mirrored black eyes, grinning with its many teeth. It was aware of his presence and he knew it, just daring him to make a move against it. And for a second there, sweat beading his brow, he thought the fucking thing was *breathing*. His own breath coming fast, Richard jabbed it with his finger, expecting it to squeak. But it made no sound. But he pulled his finger back quickly with a silent cry because...well, because the thing was soft. Soft and yielding. Not soft as in plush, but soft as in *alive*. There was no denying the hideous vitality of the thing...or its warmth. Because it *was* warm. Warm like a woman's thigh is warm. Warm like a puppy's belly or a baby's head. A living warmth, a fleshy and animate warmth.

He could not pull himself away from it.

He crouched there, sickened by the feel of the thing, the oily heat coming off it. And, yes, the sight of it. Because up close like this, he could see its patchy fur was slimed with something like jelly that had dried in snotty tangles, as if it had been pulled from a filthy Dumpster or recently crawled free of a placenta. He could smell a gamey wet-dog odor coming off it, not like the smell of a living dog but a rain-soaked dog *carcass*.

What's the matter, Richard? Do I scare you? Do I make you remember creeping things from childhood nightmares? Things that lurked in your closet and scratched down in the cellar? it seemed to say to him. *You think I'm alive and maybe I am. Maybe one dark and moonless night you'll find out just how alive I am when I slither into bed next to you and sink my teeth into your balls. Maybe I'll move right now...maybe I'll open my mouth and give you a good-night kiss and you'll feel my tongue in your mouth, only it won't feel like a tongue, but like you're French-kissing a jellyfish. Lots of maybes, Richard. Maybe you better stop worrying about what I am and start worrying about what I'm here to do, what my purpose is.*

Richard fell away, gasping for breath, going down on all fours, needing to feel the physical contact of the floor because he could feel his own world fragmenting and dissolving around him.

Behind him, he could hear the imp breathing.

He made it out into the hallway, but he did not stand or even crouch. He slid on his belly down the stairs and huddled down there in the gathering darkness, literally out of his mind.

It took him nearly an hour to come back to himself.

When he did, he screamed silently into his fist.

11

The next morning, he met Maitland for coffee.

"Well?"

Maitland looked at him for a moment after he'd sat down. "Well, I did what you asked. I parked down the street and you were right. Not fifteen minutes after you left, this old bag shows up. No car, no taxi...she just comes walking up the sidewalk. She went right past me and turned into your walk. Up the porch and in."

Richard found himself smiling. Not out of any true joy, but because, in a way, this was substantiation. No, Maitland wouldn't see it that way and no one else would either. But to Richard? Yes, substantiation, proof he wasn't mad. "Tell me about her."

Maitland just shrugged, said there wasn't much to tell. At 8:50 A.M. the old bat had gone into his house and at 11:55 A.M. she had left. Maitland hadn't hung around the rest of the day, so he couldn't say if Mrs. Crouch ever came again or not. "She was just some old lady, Richard. Kind of an odd bird, but just an old lady, I guess."

"What do you mean? How was she odd?"

"Well, this is going to sound funny…or in light of that other stuff you told me, probably not funny at all." Maitland cleared his throat, sipped his coffee. "Like I said, she was just this old lady. You wouldn't have thought twice about her if you passed her on the street, but if you watched her come and go like I did…well, you sort of noticed a few things."

Richard was waiting; he wanted to hear this.

"I've been watching people for years, Richard. Gets so you can almost tell how old someone is by their walk. Kids have a kind of bouncy, springy step to them. People in their twenties and thirties still have some of that energy, but their stride is more conservative. And when they hit middle age, they slow down. They're not in much of a hurry anymore. And elderly people? Most of 'em walk real slow, you know? Like maybe they're afraid they're going to trip and break something that won't heal again."

"What's your point, Mike?"

"My point is that this Mrs. Crouch walked fast and strong and sure for an old lady with white hair and more wrinkles than my bed."

Maitland said that struck him as funny. She was awful spry for an old lady. So spry, in fact, that at first he thought maybe she was some young woman made up *as* an old lady.

"Just funny is all," he said. "Now I'm not saying there's anything, you know, supernatural about it."

"No, of course not. Anything else funny?"

Maitland shook his head. "Not really…I mean, not unless you think it's funny for an old lady to be a headbanger."

"A headbanger?"

"Yeah, you know, heavy metal. Ozzy and Judas Priest and Metallica, that kind of thing. See, I was sitting down the street, maybe two houses down from yours, right? *Bam,* at five to twelve the old lady comes down your porch to the sidewalk, stands there like she's lost for a minute or two…then, then she turns her head real slow and looks over at where I'm parked. Shit, Richard, it was like she was looking at me, *right at me*. Gave me the fucking willies the look I saw on her face, made me shiver. Then she smiles and raises up her left hand before her face and gives me that fork-fingered sign the headbangers use at concerts. You know? With the first and pinkie finger raised and the thumb holding down the other two?"

Richard knew it, all right.

In fact, he had just read about it in his research on the Essex Witch. To most headbangers, it was probably just a cool thing to do, something invented by Ronnie James Dio. But there was a name for it and it had an interesting history. It was called the *mano cornuta* in Italy, the "devil's horns," the sign of the horned god. It was once a general symbol of the moon goddess and used in the Cult of Dagon in the Near East. Medieval devil-worshippers used it as a sign of recognition amongst their members. It was also thought to be a method of casting malice by witches, particularly when the evil eye was focused through the "horns."

Richard just sat there, feeling sick in the pit of his belly. It was ridiculous, of course, just superstition. He sipped his coffee and his hand was shaking. "Tell me something, Mike. Was…was she looking between her fingers at you?"

"Yeah…I guess she was. She didn't hold her hand up the way the headbangers do, she arched it to the side and glared at me between her fingers. Is that important?"

"I don't know, I'm not sure."

"C'mon, Richard. What is it?"

Richard was on the verge of telling him, but he just couldn't. "Holly…she made that sign, too. Just wondering what it means."

"It means it's time to dust off the old Iron Maiden records," Maitland said, not trying to be funny.

"Did you follow her, Mike?"

Maitland nodded. "From a distance, sure."

"Where did she go?"

"She kept walking right out of town, right out into the boonies. I finally had to park and tag her on foot. She led me on quite a chase, cutting through old pastureland and fields." He pulled a scrap of paper from his pocket. There was an address scrawled on it. "You know where Blassenville Road is? These days, they just call it County Road Two-Twelve. Nothing out there but—"

"Old deserted farmhouses, barns falling into themselves," Richard said, something prickling up his spine now.

"You know the place?"

"I might."

He took the slip of paper from Maitland. On it was written *17 Old Blassenville Road*. He sat there looking at it for some time without speaking. He felt weak and used-up, his stomach like a sponge that had been squeezed out. It kept rolling over on itself the way your stomach will when your sixteen-year-old daughter is late getting home and a police car rolls up the street very slowly. It might be a perfectly innocent and unrelated incident, but your mind expects the very worst.

"You've been out there, haven't you?" Maitland said.

"Yes, I have. Holly was with me. If it's the place I'm thinking of."

It's the place, you goddamn well know it's the place.

Maitland went on saying there wasn't much out on Blassenville anymore. Just all those empty farms and overgrown fields. Corporate farming had cut the throat of the family farmer. It was like that all over north-central and south-central Wisconsin, miles and miles of farmland going back to nature, all those nineteenth-century farmhouses standing dead and decrepit, looking like haunted houses being overtaken by nature. It's a shame, he said. Just a goddamn shame what corporate greed has done to the Upper Midwest, leaving much of it looking like a graveyard.

Richard said it sure was a shame.

But at that particular moment, he wasn't thinking about the plight of the family farmer or corporate predation, he was thinking about that farmhouse and the dark secrets, perhaps, boarded up in its sagging walls

He cleared his throat and said, "If it's the one I'm thinking of, it sits at the end of this winding dirt drive. Has this massive, dead-looking oak next to the house. Big sonofabitch, it would take three men to get their arms around it. Spooky-looking."

"That's the place," Maitland said. "Wanna tell me why you were there?"

Richard did. He'd always wanted to renovate one of those old dumps. You could pick them up for a song. Holly had come with him that day, a Sunday afternoon…about a month after she learned she was pregnant.

Maitland nodded. "Anyway, your Mrs. Crouch went right into that old farmhouse. I hid out in the woods for maybe an hour. She never came out, that I saw."

"You think she knew you were following her?"

"No, I was careful. She didn't have a clue."

Oh, you couldn't be that careful, Mike, Richard thought. *Not with this lady. She knew you were there, all right. Just like that sign she flashed you wasn't without meaning.*

"Anyway, that's all I got."

"You did good, Mike. Thanks."

Maitland nodded. "Anything for a pal. Can't say as how I'd want to run into that crazy-looking broad in a dark alley. She looks...I don't know, mean or something. Fucked-up, you want my opinion."

He asked Richard how things were going with Holly, and Richard bullshitted him around, telling him they were much the same.

"Well, I gotta go. You need something, you let me know." He stood up and looked down at Richard. "You know what I think that look and that finger-sign she gave me was? I think she was giving me the evil eye, putting a hex on my ass."

Richard laughed and so did Maitland, but it was obvious neither of them thought it was funny.

Maitland paused. He reached inside his coat and handed Richard something the size of a pack of cigarettes. It was thin as a cell phone. "If I were in your position, I'd get Holly on video. What you're holding is a SlimCam. Plant it in her room. It's got a thirty-two-gig card on it. It can record like twenty hours straight. Then you just plug it into the USB on your laptop and watch the video. If you get her on video, her doctor will have to do something. Get it?"

Richard did. "Thanks, Mike. I'll get it back to you."

"Keep it," Maitland said, walking away, as if maybe he hoped he'd never see him again.

12

Thinking back, Richard could remember feeling a distinct unease at the sight of the abandoned farm at 17 Blassenville Road. Holly and he were coming up the dirt drive that was flanked to either side by winter-dead thickets and ditches clotted with yellow weeds and tangled creepers. It was late March and the snows had just receded and everything was brown and still and lifeless. And cold. It was like a chill had passed through him at the sight of the place. He equated it to remembering a particularly bad dream halfway through the day, one that made you momentarily shudder. Yet there was no sense of déjà vu here, no familiarity at the sight of the old farm, just a sense of…dread.

Then it had passed equally as quick.

What both Holly and he had commented on first was the enormous lightning-blasted oak just to the side of the farmhouse itself. It was easily a hundred feet high and anchored by a stout trunk that radiated out into a knotted mass of craggy limbs and spidery branches. Seeing it, Richard thought it looked like a skeletal hand reaching up to claw at the gray sky above. There was something brooding and ominous about that tree. It looked terribly threatening, almost as if it were possessed of some malefic life, a dreaming and diseased sentience in the skeletal reach of the branches or the anguished twist of the trunk or the convoluted bark itself.

Like it was watching them arrive and wanting to crush them.

Even Holly had remarked on it. "Have you ever seen such a…a horrid-looking tree?"

Richard admitted he hadn't.

It looked like the sort of gnarled and sinewy oak that might have been used as a hanging tree in the old days. An arboreal gallows. He could almost imagine those knotty and serpentine limbs with nooses hanging from them, highwaymen and cut-throats swinging in the breeze, rotating from side-to-side with an abhorrent slowness, limbs creaking and wind howling through the high branches above. That's what he had thought and thinking it, he was reminded that he had read once that such hanging trees were thought to absorb the souls of the executed, their agony and madness. There was no getting around the fact that this particular oak looked tormented.

"We buy this place," Richard said, "and that tree's coming down."

"Yeah…it's spooky," Holly admitted. "Gives me the creeps for some reason. I can just imagine the shadows it would throw. Brrr."

Richard had told her that was not why—even though it was, partly—but because if a good storm knocked it over, it would go right into the house. Split the roof asunder. That sounded good at the time; better than the truth.

The farmhouse itself looked no worse than others on Blassenville. Richard knew looking at it that it was probably of mid-nineteenth-century construction. A typical Midwestern frame house, two-story, with elaborate jigsaw trim that had mostly rotted away, a wraparound farmer's porch and scroll gables, narrow windows that were either boarded-over now or shattered in their frames. It was in poor condition, all in all, most of the shingles blown free from the low-pitched roof, walls sagging, porch overhang ready to collapse, shutters askew if extant at all. It looked its age, weathered and ruined, just waiting to fall. The sort of place kids might gather by candlelight on windy October nights to tell ghost stories.

Even the high, brick-ended plank barn was riddled with holes, the roof caved in on the far side, its doors bowed in their frames. Everything warped by too many harsh Wisconsin winters and hot summers.

No, Richard had thought, *just too far gone.*

And yet, they had gone inside.

Even later that day, he was astounded by this. He had dragged a pregnant woman into that derelict like he was asking for the both of them to be buried alive in timbers 150 years old, entombed in the rubble. But, truth be told, it wasn't all that bad inside—dirty, dusty, full of birds' nests and rodent droppings, a carpeting of brown leaves blown in through holes in the walls—but structurally sound. Made to last in a climate that was notoriously punishing. The rooms were uniformly boxy, the flowery wallpaper long faded. Great holes were rotted through the walls, cobwebbed slats on display. There was no furniture. Even the kitchen cupboards and plumbing fixtures were gone.

Just another ruined farmhouse...yet, it seemed to be so much more.

Richard was struck by something far worse than that feeling he'd had on the road in. This was enveloping and total, making his guts wind into corkscrews and filling his mouth with a taste like rusting iron. The house was soundless, dead and vacant like a pile of bones.

Holly said: "Gotta love this atmosphere. Like a fucking morgue."

He had laughed.

Not because it was funny, really (it wasn't) but because she was right. Being inside there was like being inside the carcass of an animal that had had the blood sucked from it drop by drop until there was nothing left but skeleton and skin.

"Can we go now before the Crypt Keeper shows up?" Holly asked.

"Ha, ha."

They went back outside, both grateful to breathe in the fresh air of the day, grateful to be free of the ominous, enclosing coffinlike atmosphere of the farmhouse. Hand in hand, they walked through the yellow grasses out near the barn. Just beyond was a low brick building that almost seemed to be sinking into the earth.

"It must be where the Keebler elves live," Holly said.

She was trying hard to be funny, to cancel out the bleak, almost pestilent atmosphere that came from the building. If the farmhouse had been oppressive, this place was almost sickening in its misery and desolation. It made Richard's belly feel hollow.

"It's a piggery," he heard himself say.

"A *what?*"

"A piggery. *Was* a piggery. A pigsty," he said. "This would have been where they kept the hogs when this place was operating."

Holly just stared at it. "Makes my skin crawl."

Richard felt the same way, but he refused to give in to it. The idea was ridiculous. He went up to the building and peered into the low dusty and broken windows. There was a set of green, peeling doors at the front and even though Holly told him to leave it be, he forced them open and a hot, deeply entrenched animal stink blew out at him. It was there and then it was gone.

"I'm going to have a look," he said.

"Please, Richard. It doesn't look safe."

But that wasn't what she was afraid of and it wasn't what he was afraid of either. If the farm had a black, beating heart, then it was here in the depths of the piggery and he planned on tracking it to its source even though, somehow, he knew it was a very bad idea.

Just inside the doorway, there was a well-trod dirt run that sloped down farther into the earth. He followed it into the bowels of the building. To either side were brick sty pens, long disused. What light came in through the windows was dirty and discolored, its stray beams nearly clotted with whirling specks of dust. He followed the run deeper, ancient hay crunching under his step. It smelled dank, dark, and subterranean in there. Shadows moved around him, darkness spilling out of the pens like blood from slit veins.

He thought that if those doors above were suddenly to slam shut, he would scream. It was irrational as all hell, but he had thought it. There was a rising stink that was low and mean, the smell of animal droppings, of peeled hides, of birth and slaughter and blood.

It was at that moment that it got worse.

"Richard?" he heard Holly cry out. "Oh, Richard...answer me."

The air was suddenly redolent with the foul, acrid stench of pig shit and filthy straw. He could hear the communal buzz of dung flies feeding upon it. He could sense things moving in the pens themselves, rolling in the mud and excrement. His face beaded with a cold/hot sweat of fear, the stench thick as grease in his throat, he had an inexplicable, almost obscene desire to step into one of the pens. To peel off his shoes and socks and wade into the filth, feel the oozing foulness of it between his toes and know its heat and depths, sink in the rank pools of fly-specked muck and ordure where the fleshy, bulky forms of hogs rolled like fetuses in hot, juicy wombs.

"RICHARD!"

Not a summons, but a shriek of fear. It was like a slap across the face. Blinking, he looked around, seeing nothing but abandoned pens, deep dry hollows in them where the pigs had snorted happily in their mud and shit, gnawed on their slop. Even the smell was gone.

Holly cried out again and he ran up and out of the piggery.

She was gasping, doubled over, clutching her belly, driven right to her knees in the dirt. Richard took hold of her right away, scared silly.

"Holly? Oh Jesus, Holly, are you okay?"

"Yes," she said breathing very hard. "A pain…God, I had a shooting pain in my belly." She breathed in and out. "Why didn't you answer?"

"I'm sorry…I don't know."

He helped her to her feet and her forehead was damp with sweat. She told him she was fine and he wanted to believe her, but she looked scared. Really scared.

"Let's just get out of this place," she said.

And that's just what they did.

It was on the way out, as he got Holly into the SUV, that he heard something from the direction of the farmhouse that chilled him for days afterward. Old houses are notorious for the sounds they can create. Loose boards creak, ancient foundations settle, attic beams groan in the wind. They make lots of sounds, but Richard was pretty sure they were incapable of making the sound he heard as he climbed in next to Holly. The sound that sent him racing away down the drive, spraying gravel.

Sow

Squealing.
The delighted squealing of a pig.

13

It was child's play planting the SlimCam.

He brought the hag her lunch of raw meat and secreted the unit between a vase of flowers and a digital clock on the dresser. She never even paid attention to him, carrying on some whispering conversation with what was growing in her belly. The imp grinned at him as if it knew what he was up to, but then it always grinned like a wind-up monkey.

He didn't leave until she hissed at him and by then, the SlimCam was already recording.

14

Later that afternoon, he did some thinking.

If he'd been looking for a connection, then there it was. It hadn't occurred to him to equate that weird day in the farmhouse five months before with what was happening to his wife here and now. He'd pretty much forgotten about the farmhouse and the piggery, his weird experience in the pens and the weird pain Holly had suffered. And as much as that squealing had unnerved him at the time, in the coming days he could not be sure just what he had heard. *Squealing?* No, certainly not. There hadn't been a living pig there in decades. So, being modern and rational, he'd reached out for that oldest and most clichéd of explanations: *it was just the wind*. Just the wind blowing through a hole in the roof and getting into the walls, bouncing around in there, channeling through crevices and creating a sound *like* squealing...but surely not *actual* squealing.

The idea was ludicrous.

Except it didn't seem so ludicrous now.

Thinking it over, staring at the burning end of his cigarette, Richard was connecting everything to that day. He still wasn't sure where Mrs. Crouch factored in (other than the fact that she was a reincarnated sixteenth-century witch...heh, heh), but the rest was very clear to him. Through some arcane influence, something had been planted in Holly that day. It was not rape as such, because she had already been pregnant. But he was of a mind that their child had died that day and been replaced with something else. It made perfect sense to him as delusions always did to madmen, he supposed.

Up until that day, Richard, he told himself, *you were a proud father. Your son or daughter was growing happily in Holly's womb and then...then something invaded it, something sucked the life from your baby. Something like a sentient tumor. Something that has been waiting to be born for centuries.*

No! Stop it, this is going too far now.

Shut up and listen, bright boy.

What's growing in your wife's womb is not natural nor human. It's no more a baby than that baboon/toad thing is a teddy bear. But like it, it's deranged and diabolic, something without a soul. Something the good Lord intended to keep in the darkness where it belonged. Something coiling and repellent that was meant to crawl in the webby subcellar of the cosmos, not walk in full daylight. You just keep that in mind, all right? Because the time might come when you have the chance to save the world from it, when you find it alone and defenseless and you can get your hands around its slimy neck—

Enough, by God, that was enough.

He stood straight up, breathing hard and balling his hands into fists. He was not a killer. He was not a savior. It was not his place to kill children, to cleanse evil from the world. He didn't care what that thing—or things—was, he was not going to kill it.

Not children, you moron. It may creep from your wife's womb dressed out in flesh and blood, but it sure as hell won't be a child. No child in history had a dark, ravening mind like this thing, a mind that was ancient when the stars were young.

Just remember, whatever's in her belly took your child. It devoured your son or your daughter so that it might be born. Show it no more mercy than it showed your baby.

Understand?

If what the hag says is correct, there will be many of them. Parasites. Treat them as such. Cleanse the world of them.

Richard was beginning to imagine what it would all be like. Holly would die in childbirth, but that seed in her would live. At least until he got his hands on it—or *them*—and twisted its revolting little head from its body. Then he would be placed in a padded room for the rest of his life with all the other saviors. And wasn't that just a real fucking rosy outlook on the future?

Sighing, not knowing where to turn, he went upstairs.

He had never felt more alone or more vulnerable in his life.

At the door to Holly's room—funny how it was no longer *his* room—he paused and for the first time in he didn't know how long, prayed. He prayed to whoever would listen and he actually meant it.

He stepped inside.

Holly was sleeping.

She was sprawled over the bed, a graying sheet wound around her like a shroud. Her distended belly was spilled out on the mattress like Santa's goody bag...but there were no goodies in there, only salivating, leggy things coming to term like fetal spiders in egg sacs. Holly's face did not look peaceful even in sleep. It was bruised and puffy, shadows under the eyes, a line of drool hanging from her chin.

Richard stood there, staring at her, fighting the tears that came.

He turned around suddenly, feeling Pigwicken staring at him, his eyes like open wounds. Knowing he was being watched, feeling those distant and forbidding eyes on him, Richard drew his finger across his throat, thinking, *I'm suffering now…but later? Your time will come, oh yes, be assured of that, you ugly prick. I'll have the last laugh for the defilement of my wife and my baby.*

He turned and looked at the SlimCam.

Then at Holly.

The corner of her lips turned up in something like a scowl. A dirty, almost mildewed stink came off her. It was stronger and more corrupt, for some reason, when she was sleeping, but it wasn't exactly mouth-watering when she was awake either.

He kneeled next to the bed.

Carefully, he touched his fingertips against the swollen white mound of her belly. Pregnant women's bellies were very taut, very hard like they had been inflated to the point of bursting. Holly's was no different. Richard felt a tear roll down his face as he pressed his hand flat to her stomach. Her flesh was hot, feverish. An odd salty smell came from it.

Something moved under his hand.

Something *kicked*.

Many things kicked, actually.

He tensed, felt sickened. Yes, like they really *were* fetal spiders moving in egg sacs. It was that appalling, that offensive. He wanted to take a knife and stab the life brooding in the hot darkness. There was more movement and then it ceased. Maybe it knew an unfriendly and threatening hand when it felt one.

Holly stirred, but did not waken.

Richard, not really knowing why, brought his head down and pressed it to her belly, feeling that he should. Like a kid poking something disgusting with a stick, the sense of curiosity was overwhelming. His ear was against her warm belly now. At first he could hear nothing but the usual gastric processes…rumbling and sluicing.

But then he heard something else.

He pulled his head away, chewing on his lower lip so he didn't cry out. There was no mistaking what he had heard: voices. The sound of many voices whispering.

He stumbled from the room before his mind completely went.

15

The next morning there was a knock at the door.

Richard answered it, half-awake, still wiping sleep from his eyes. Holly's Uncle Dick and Aunt Pauline were there. They'd just come from church, thought they had better stop by to see how Holly was doing.

"Well, come on in," Richard told them. "I just put the coffee on."

He ushered them into the living room, told them both to sit down and brought them both cups of coffee. He honestly wasn't sure whether them stopping by was a good thing or a bad thing. It was funny, but he almost felt like he had to hide Holly from the world. She was a dirty secret he coveted and had to protect…like a blow-up doll in the closet or a woman chained up in the basement. As if, had they found out the truth, it would make him look like some sort of deviant, a criminal.

Aunt Pauline touched her lacquered, fire-red beehive. "You sleeping okay, Richard? You look a little on the rough side, you don't mind me saying so."

"Ah…I…I had a few of the boys over last night. Played some cards, you know."

Uncle Dick laughed until his belly shook. "Yeah, well I *used* to know," he said, jabbing a thumb at his wife. "That was a good thirty years ago, though. You win anything?"

"No, lost my ass."

"You got my luck then. Lost my paycheck once…but let's not talk about that," he said.

"Oh, Dick," Pauline said. She turned to Richard. "I thought I smelled smoke in here. Secondhand smoke is bad for babies, they say. At least that's what I heard on TV."

"Shit," Uncle Dick said. "I had a ciggie hanging from my mouth when George was born, when they brought me in the room."

"That was forty years ago, Dick."

"So what's the difference? You listen to them health Nazis, you might as well roll over and die now. They take all the fun out of life."

Aunt Pauline shrugged. "Course, both of my children were X-rayed. Didn't have ultrasounds back then. They used to X-ray mothers. Two, three times during your pregnancy. My kids turned out all right, though. They're perfectly normal."

Dick started laughing. "Normal, *hell*. Linda lives with another woman. You call that normal? Jesus H. Christ."

"Dick…"

"Hey, Richard, the little mother up or is she still sawing logs?"

That was a good question. Richard knew how easily it would have been to lie his way out of it, but why? What did he owe that hag upstairs? Might as well put her on the spot.

He jogged upstairs and threw open the door to Holly's room.

The hag sat there, glaring at him, eyes winking like dying suns. "I want some food, Richard. You will bring me some food."

Richard just smiled.

Whatever was possessing his wife was not that smart, after all. It was hardly the all-seeing, all-knowing sage he'd thought it to be. It didn't even know there were guests in the house.

"You awake?" he said. "Good." He turned from the door and shouted out into the hallway: "C'mon up, she's awake!"

The thing on the bed glared lividly at him.

It was no longer Holly at all, just something bloated and coiling that wormed its way from a waste heap…and died with the exertion.

He walked over to the window and slid it up. The pane was fanned out with cracks, but it was in no real danger of shattering. "Here. This is what you need, dear, some fresh September air."

He turned back and the hag was gone.

Holly, *his* Holly was sitting on the bed. Her cheeks were rosy and those awful teeth were gone. Even her silver eyes had given way to blue. Amazing. And this in a matter of seconds, mere seconds.

"Yes, the air smells wonderful, Richard," she said.

Jesus, even the voice was different.

And something else…the imp was gone.

Uncle Dick and Aunt Pauline were coming up the steps now, Dick complaining all the way up about how stairs killed him these days, how he just didn't have the wind for it. Too many years smoking, he said. Pauline told him the fifty extra pounds weren't helping either. They were still arguing about it when they reached the doorway.

"Ha, ha," Uncle Dick said, "lookit the girl there! The picture of health!"

Holly smiled, turning on the juice, as lovely as lovely got. "Never felt better."

Richard just stood there, grinding his molars.

This was more disturbing than anything else—the way she could turn it on and off. Was it even possible for someone to undergo physical change that quickly? What sort of cellular mastery would you have to have to make it happen? No matter. Because it would be on the SlimCam now. For posterity.

Aunt Pauline went over and kissed Holly on the cheek. "How you doing, honey?"

"Oh, just fine," Holly said. "I'm getting a little tired of being bedridden, but I'm catching up on my reading."

She smiled at Richard.

Yes, she was catching up on her reading, all right. There was a stack of books over on the shelf. Most of them were leather-bound and very old, filled with words Richard couldn't even begin to translate. He had a feeling those books were probably worth a fortune, didn't exist anywhere outside of special university library collections.

"Well?" Uncle Dick asked. "Have you decided?"

Richard had no idea what he was talking about, but then he remembered that just before Holly began to change they'd been fussing over names as all new parents did. Boys' names, girls' names. It all seemed ages ago now.

"We're still discussing it, aren't we, Richard?"

Richard just stared at her. "I was thinking *Damien*."

"Oh, good God. That's a terrible name," Aunt Pauline said. "Sounds like the Antichrist or something. Yuck."

Now Richard was the one smiling.

Holly was not amused in the least.

"You know," Uncle Dick said, "I still lean towards 'Richard.' Then you could call the kid 'Little Richard.'" He started laughing over that one. "But, really, why not? *Richard*. Then his friends could call him 'Dick.' Not that I'm biased in that direction, you understand. My old man was named

'Richard,' just like me and like you, Richard. When I was a kid, he was Big Dick and I was Little Dick, Little Dicky."

"You'll always be Little Dicky to me," Pauline said.

Uncle Dick just nodded, like she'd paid him a compliment.

Christ, this entire situation was surreal. Aunt Pauline was practicing her usual dry wit and it was all going right over her husband's head. And Holly…what *she* was, it was going right over *both* of their heads. There was something terribly demented about all this, too many levels on the playing field. Richard wondered what sort of things he was missing here. Aunt Pauline kept right on rolling, asking Holly if she ever called Richard "Big Dick." Still, it was lost on her husband. Usually, Richard and Holly were breaking up over this. But not now. Holly was smiling, but there was a darkness hiding just behind her eyes waiting to insinuate itself and Richard saw it.

"We're very happy," Holly said. "Aren't we, Richard?"

Truth or lie? "Yes," Richard managed. "Happy as horseshit."

Uncle Dick laughed.

Aunt Pauline raised an eyebrow, intuiting, as women tended to, a bit of stress between her niece and her husband. "Richard? Why is that window open? It's barely sixty degrees out there this morning. Last thing you want is Holly catching a cold."

"Yes, Richard," Holly said.

"See how they gang up?" Uncle Dick said, winking at him. "You get some hens together and they'll peck a rooster to death."

"Oh, Dick…really," Aunt Pauline said.

Richard closed the window, hoping Holly's aunt and uncle would comment on the spiderwebbed pane, but they did not.

Uncle Dick said, "It's going to be quite a change, eh, Richard? Having a baby around the house."

Richard only nodded.

Holly smiled…or tried to, but smiling was no longer natural to her. "Oh, but we're looking forward to it…aren't we, Richard? We're looking forward to bringing junior into the world. I'm hoping he looks just like his father."

"Isn't that sweet?" Aunt Pauline said.

But she looked over at Richard and it was obvious she didn't believe that. Maybe she knew her niece and maybe she was just perceptive and slightly clairvoyant like most women, but she had picked up on something. And right then she was worrying it over in her mind. Richard was watching her closely and she was watching Holly closely. And the SlimCam watched all.

"Is something wrong, Auntie?" Holly said.

Aunt Pauline just kept staring at her. "I don't know, dear…*is* there?"

Holly offered her that world-winning smile, all those perfect, even white teeth and those wonderful blue eyes. She looked like a varsity cheerleader: healthy, flawless, and happy, full of life. "Of course not. We've never been happier, have we, Richard?"

He smiled thinly, but didn't comment.

Uncle Dick patted his belly. "Well, I'm glad we got that shit sorted out." He rolled his eyes at Richard and Richard knew he was thinking, *women*. He patted his belly again. "All right, Pauline, let's go get some breakfast. My stomach's asking me if my throat's been cut here."

Holly laughed. "Same old Uncle Dick."

They said their good-byes and both kissed Holly on the cheeks, Aunt Pauline saying how she wished her sister, Eileen, was here to see this. Eileen had been Holly's mom. Both of Holly's parents had died in an auto accident ten years before. Holly didn't like to talk about them much.

Richard walked Uncle Dick and Aunt Pauline downstairs and Uncle Dick clapped him on the shoulder and went out the door, making for his car in the driveway. Aunt Pauline, however, lingered.

She put a hand on Richard's arm. "Is everything all right?"

"Sure," he lied. "Just fine."

She looked into his eyes and knew it wasn't so. "You can tell me, Richard. Really, you can."

No, I can't. You and Dick are wonderful people. I couldn't destroy you with the truth.

"It's just...well, things have been a little strained lately. I suppose we're under stress."

"Hey!" Uncle Dick called from outside. "Let's make for some grub here! I think I'm starting to lose weight!"

Aunt Pauline ignored him. "You're a terrible liar, Richard." She turned, then stopped in the doorway. "Anytime you need me, honey, I'm only a phone call away."

Then she was out the door and into the car.

Richard watched them pull away. He just stood there, waving, but inside he was trembling and crying, just totally heartbroken.

16

He went back upstairs.

He had nearly twenty hours of video on the SlimCam, but that wasn't what brought him up there. There was violence in his mind. Deadly, razor-edged violence that was cutting deep. He was going to kill her. If Holly had reverted to that hag again, he was going to wrap his hands around her sallow, corded throat and squeeze the grotesque life from her.

That's what he was going to do.

That's exactly what he was going to do.

He'd been pushed too far and he was crazy, he knew he was crazy, and he was going to put an end to it once and for all. Because if he didn't, then what was coming to term in Holly's belly would not only go after him it would go after Uncle Dick and Aunt Pauline. Two perfectly wonderful people. It would do horrendous things to them, it would degrade and destroy them in ways he could not allow.

No, the witch was going to die, and when he was done with her, he'd take his own life. Yes, yes, it all seemed perfectly reasonable in his delirious mind.

When he got to the door, he threw it open, and as he did so, thoughts of homicide vanished from his mind. The room was an envelope of heat and misery. It smelled like piss and excrement and rot. The first thing he became aware of were the flies. They were everywhere. They lit in clouds in the air. They crawled up the cracked windowpane. They were thick as fur on the walls, buzzing and swarming. One crawled across his cheek, another settled on the back of his hand.

It smelled as the piggery had smelled that weird, hallucinogenic day at the abandoned farm.

Yes, and why not? The room *was* a sty…the floor a swamp of pig shit, blood, filthy straw, and the accumulated remains of slop: the tiny red-stained bones of children, shanks of well-gnawed meat, nibbled ropes of entrails. The smell was moist, steaming, and perfectly nauseating. Worms wriggled in it. Beetles scurried through it. It was like the collected fetid guano of a bat colony. Moving. Shivering. Stinking.

Then Richard looked at what was on the bed.

His breath rattling dry in his throat, he saw it was neither the hag nor his wife, but what looked like the formidable girth of a well-fed sow whose flanks were speckled with mud and excrement. She had the hooves of a swine, but human hands that she brushed along her pink, glossy porcine flesh. Flies crawled over her. Gray ticks swollen with blood hung like fat seeds from her underbelly as she rolled over and exposed the rows of milk-bloated teats. She spread her legs so he could see the oily vaginal slit and the meat flies that peppered it.

"Lay with me, Richard," she said in some perverse mockery of Holly's voice. "Melt into me, my lover. Drown in my sweetness. Let me squeal for you."

He stared speechlessly at her imposing pink girth, the mounded teats spilling milk, the slimy cleft between her legs from which legions of wriggling silverfish squirmed free to play on her pale, weighty thighs. She held a hand out to him and the fingers were uniformly plump, the nails yellowed and stubby.

He was revolted.

The hag had been bad enough, but this…this hybrid swine, this great lolling sow, inviting him to lie with her in the pig-house stink of the marriage bed she had duly anointed with her own piss, shit, and numerous contaminated secretions…no, it was beyond horror, it was beyond anything as abstract as madness…it was a degradation and a depravity that sucked the blood from the soft white underbelly of his soul with pulsing lips.

He found that he was not so much looking around the room, but *feeling* around it in his mind, testing the physical reality of it. The entire episode had a surreal, dreamlike quality to it. He was certain of nothing. Not the four walls or the floor beneath his feet. Any of it could dissipate or fold up at any moment.

You can't be seeing this. It's a trick. A witch's trick. She's playing you again and you're falling for it.

"There's no trick, Richard," the sow promised him. "Take my hand and I'll make it all better."

Part of him did not doubt that she would. Lying with her would be the final violation of all that he was…yet he almost wanted it. He sought the cool darkness of destruction she offered. Outwardly, yes, he was revolted, but inwardly, in the depths of his subconscious, he was hearing her siren call and wanting badly to answer it.

He stared down at the pink perfection of her skin and found himself wanting to sink into her depths, to feel that ravening snout at his throat, that coarse tongue at his belly, the blunt bristles beneath his fingertips. She was seduction and obscenity personified and made truth. Flies lit on his face as she grinned at him and he felt his hand rising to clasp her own. He could already feel her moist, chubby digits encircling his fingers as she drew him down, down to the marriage bed and the coital entwining. He could feel her flab beneath his hands and taste the salty brine of her pig-sweat upon his lips as she grunted happily.

But no.

He backed away. It would not be that easy for her. He wouldn't let it be.

She tittered. "In the end, Richard, you'll give me what I want. You won't have a choice. You'll bring what is mine and offer it freely."

He stumbled from the room and went downstairs. There in the silence, he listened to the screams inside his own head.

17

Later, he came back, stinking of whiskey and cigarettes. He kicked open the door and stumbled in there, knowing that in death there was life and in purification there was freedom…so he booted the door open with murder on his mind and the sty was still there. As were the flies and mud and globs of feces, the bubbling carpet of carrion and hog-slop. Just as were the walls the swine had anointed with her acrid piss.

"Richard," she said, "have you no respect for privacy."

"You bitch," he said, "you filthy, stinking, murdering bitch."

The swine was amused by him as perhaps she had always been amused. When he tried to edge closer, to snatch the grime-streaked sheet from her body, she snorted and squealed at him with that guttural, boarlike growling. She was getting angry. Her eyes were bleary with venom. Her snout peeled back to reveal rows of yellow, nubby teeth made for tearing and grinding.

But that wasn't what stopped him.

It was an image she placed in his head. It could have come from nowhere else. It flashed in his mind like some cheap, sordid, and grisly grindhouse trailer: her well-fattened thighs spread, her blubbery privates greased with pig-slime, one hand up inside herself to the wrist. What she pulled out was not the horror she would soon birth to an unsuspecting world, but *his* child. *His* son. *His* daughter. It was a pink and perfect fetus still dripping with placental fluid from the sheared birth sac. She held it up by the ankles, a coiled umbilical like the tail of a hog connecting it to her.

She dangled the squealing, helpless child like a strip of bacon.

Then…then as it played through his mind, the sow grinned at him, flashing those teeth that gleamed like untried razor blades. A porcine tongue thick and meaty licked them.

In his mind, he screamed.

Her snout darted in, tearing out soft pink bites of flesh from the child, opening its belly and laying its throat raw until her snout was dipped red. Lastly, she seized its head in her jaws and chomped down, cracking it open like a walnut. The sound was that of an ice cube crunched in teeth.

It was only an image, but one, he knew, she could breathe with reality anytime she so chose.

She lay back against her pillows, grinning like a boar. There was activity beneath the sheet, a movement and a sound like a baby sucking on a bottle. Slowly then, she pulled it away, exposing herself. He gazed at her swollen pink mass that was flecked with crawling vermin. Shit leaked from her flanks. Her pendulant tits were swollen with milk. Cradled there in her arm, nestled in the rows of veined teats, was the imp, Pigwicken. Its baboon snout was suckling one of the tits, working it with a wet and slobbering suction, gulping down hot mother's milk. One of the familiar's eyes circled dreamily in its orbit, staring out at him with an erotic thrill.

"As it is," said the swine, "so it shall be. Soon, those of true faith will be called upon to give unto me what is mine by birthright."

18

And still later, he returned again, but only to take the SlimCam away with him. It took hours to get his stomach under control and to build up the nerve to climb the stairs. The sty was gone. Holly was the hag again, fingers gone to marbled sausages and limbs distended and belly rounded, fat pocketed by fat, a huge and heaving construction of oily white meat. She shivered and perspired heavily in her sleep.

Her familiar squatted with its eyes closed now. It was making a low bleating sound that was quite near snoring.

Richard grabbed up the SlimCam and left the room, making his way down to the living room, still feeling the slow crawl of Pigwicken's alien eyes upon him. They had been shut, yet he was certain they watched as they always watched. If it knew what he was up to, then the hag would know soon enough. It seemed absurd to be thinking of that grotesque moppet as a sentient being, but it was. Somehow and some way, that thing was a watchdog with a cunning, evil brain.

Breathing so fast he thought he might hyperventilate, Richard plugged the SlimCam USB into his laptop, downloaded the software prompt, and within minutes was watching the video. The beginning was pretty boring, but the unit captured everything that happened and it was enough, more than enough, to prove his wife was no longer his wife but a wizened monstrosity. The best stuff was that of he himself talking to the hag and she snarling off at him, then Uncle Dick and Aunt Pauline coming into the room…seconds before they did, the hag changed back into Holly. Pretty, healthy, blue-eyed Holly. It was no slow Lon Chaney type of transformation or even a high-tech CGI morphing. It happened as quickly as a shadow passing over the hag's face. That fast. That unbelievable. And also that incontrovertible.

God damn you, you fucking witch, Richard thought, feeling strong for the first time in days. *I got you now and when they see this, you'll be confined to a madhouse until you release your grip on my wife. Your young will go into specimen jars to be dissected, pickled, and labeled as the freaks they are.*

These were the things that went through his head as he watched the footage.

Then something happened.

The video rolled like the image from an old TV set. It blurred. It flickered. And then, and then—

And then it was no longer video of the bedroom. No, it was grainy footage of the piggery at the old farm. It could be nowhere else, he realized, as his heart clenched like a fist. As in his hallucination that day—if that's what it had been—the piggery appeared to be in full operation. There was mud in the sties, piles of hay, straw on the floor, buckets of slop set about. The image panned from pen to pen to pen. They were all empty save for the one at the end. Something immense and fleshy rolled in the mud.

It was the swine.

Of course, it was the swine.

Because that porcine horror was the root of it all and the hag was nothing but a mask, a kiddie spook-show interpretation of her true reality. Simple imagery for simple minds. Slicked in black mud, the swine rose from the pool. She stood on her rear trotters, her teats fully exposed, droplets of dirty black water dripping from them. She was no mindless, dumb farm animal waiting to be processed into pork and ham, she was omnipotent and divine and demanded like treatment. This was the creature that had possessed Alizon Clove into seducing Jane Penden as a perspective mother. The squealing young that would have come to term in her belly were now safely planted in the nursery of Holly, growing and thriving.

Richard looked upon her, his guts going weak.

Though she was well-fattened, rounded in every way, he could see the enormous bulge of her pregnancy quite clearly. She ran her hands over the mound of gestating life proudly. Grinning lewdly, her translucent yellow eyes staring at the camera, her distended teats, oiled flanks, and bulging loins were on full display. He could almost smell the hot brine of her swelling vulva, hear the hissing escape of gas from her hind quarters and her hoglike snaffling and grunting.

She was no mere witch or sorceress, she was beyond that—a primal image, a fertility goddess, a dawn effigy, the mother archetype rendered in pink porky flesh. She was fertile and hot, vital and juicy with child, her parts engorged with estrus. Her field had been long ago plowed and seeded by Old Jack Hobb, her wriggling crops raised under exacting conditions and the yield would be rich.

Richard knew things then. He could feel her thoughts spearing into his own, her dominance filling his brain in a black-seeking corruption, leeching him and teaching him the old ways. He knew that just as Holly's body had been selected as a proper vessel—and her/their child torn free like a bothersome parasitic weed, replaced with some nameless ancient incubation—he had also been selected. He would not be the first human male she had used, broken, and discarded. There had been many, legions of them. All of it, from beginning to end, was about fertility. It was the circle of life. She took men to drain them of seed. She devoured her own young. She tore living human fetuses from bloody wombs as sacrifice and castrated her own lovers in her jealousy so they could share their male ripeness with no other. These offerings were made willingly to her. To submit was agony; to deny, an ordeal legendary in its horror.

The video flickered.

He saw an old man and old woman, both naked and pouchy with age. Their pale skins looked blotchy and diseased in comparison to the pink vibrancy of the swine. They carried buckets and splashed the contents on the mother sow. She accepted this with a heated squealing: entrails, blood, and organ meats. They were slopping her with human waste.

Then Richard saw a row of children being herded forward, boys all. Each naked. Each innocent. One by one they lay on their backs, spreading their legs and offering her the immature fruit of their loins that she so desired. On all fours, she sniffed at the offerings, licking and teasing and nipping before her jaws clamped down and chewed the fruit to bloody rind.

That's where the video ended.

Richard sat there, swooning with a cool white terror in his head, the room pitching and lilting around him. But he understood. He understood what she was and what she expected.

19

It was nearly two in the morning when the call came.

"Richard," Maitland said. "I found out some things I need to share with you."

Richard, numb and defeated, merely said, "I'm listening."

Maitland didn't say anything for a time. He just breathed on the line. "I did some digging. That farmhouse. It's been empty since the mid-Seventies. It's got kind of a bad reputation, if you know what I mean."

"Haunted?" Richard said. "Is that what you're saying?"

"I guess, I don't know. Back in seventy-four, there was this old couple that died there. Name of Elder. Tom and Bridget Elder. He killed her with a shotgun, then turned it on himself. No note, no nothing. But I did find out from a friend of mine, a state cop, that there's was something just plain weird about that house, what they found there."

"How so?"

"Well, I guess they found some books, Richard. Not the kind of books your wife has...not exactly. These were big homemade-looking books, my guy tells me. They had pictures of the old woman, except a lot younger. Pictures of her standing around naked..."

There was nothing pornographic exactly about the pictures, Maitland said. Not really. Just pictures of Bridget Elder with kids. Boys, always boys. Just Bridget Elder and a series of naked boys with the same blank look on their faces. They had been photographed in the old pigsties. But as to what the significance of that was, no one could say. None of the boys could be positively identified using the photos. As to whether they were locals or missing and exploited children, it was anyone's guess.

None of this came as any surprise to Richard, of course. He knew many things he could not bring himself to speak of. *They would have been twelve or thirteen years old, Mike, all of them. Boys who were sexually maturing, going through puberty, but not quite mature. Their fruit would be ripe but not well-seasoned the way the sow likes it. Virgins all. She would accept nothing less. They would have been given as offerings to her. Each of them would have given themselves voluntarily or maybe* been *given voluntarily by their families, all of whom would have been farmers, agricultural types tied to the land whose blood ran dark and deep, rich as the black Midwestern soil itself. The very idea of that is obscene, but what we're dealing with is a pagan survival, an ancient fertility cult, definitely European, possibly Neolithic in origin, that was practiced for certain in Essex County, England, in the sixteenth century. Those peasant farmers would have made expiation in the purest Old Testament sense to the swine and Old Jack Hobb. And somehow, it's still going on. That's the core of this entire thing: the past haunting the present and damning the future. A corruption born in antiquity has seeded itself in my wife and killed my baby and, God help us, but hell is about to come into this world—*

"When I walked away from you at the coffee shop the other day," Maitland said, "I wanted to wash my hands of this whole thing. I didn't like any of it. I didn't like what you told me and you know what? I liked it even less how that crazy old bat Mrs. Crouch made me feel when she looked at me. I bullshitted around with you, Richard, but the truth was…that bitch *scared* me. When she looked at me that day, I thought I was going to piss my pants."

"I feel that way every time I look at my wife," Richard admitted.

"I'll just bet you do." Maitland sighed. "I don't know what's going on here, but I got a real bad gut-feeling, old buddy. And it's not just what you said…I don't know what it is exactly…but my nerves have been on edge since the other day. I'm…I'm having real bad dreams here. Thing is, I'm not so sure they're dreams."

"What do you mean, Mike?" Richard was feeling scared again. And this time it was not for himself.

Maitland cleared his throat. Richard could hear him light a cigarette on the other end. Maitland, like Richard, hadn't smoked in years. "I keep…oh this is fucking crazy…but I keep waking up in the dead of night, you know? I sleep like a goddamn baby. Always have. But I been waking up and, Christ, Richard, I keep thinking somebody's in the apartment here with me. I thought…I thought somebody was *standing* next to my bed the other night, somebody was leaning over me, breathing on me. Jesus, I know how nutty this sounds. Maybe I got a fever going or something. But I woke up gasping like I was choking. I was having this dream that…that Mrs. Crouch had her mouth on mine and she was sucking the breath out of my lungs."

He said there was more than just that.

He always kept his door shut. Just a habit he picked up as a kid, and every morning his door was open. And the night of that suffocation dream, the window in his bedroom was also open. But he hadn't opened it. He never opened it unless it was the dog days of summer and it had been chilly of late.

"I'm losing it, Richard," he said.

But Richard didn't think he was.

Maitland was tough. He'd played football in college, pulled four years in the Marines after that. He was a brave guy, dragged his balls around in a wheelbarrow they were so goddamn big. The guy was iron. But now? Putty. Nothing but soft, pliant putty. He had been broken. He was scared and Richard was scared for him.

"Last night…I got in late and there was this stink in the apartment. I don't know…like a squirrel had died in the walls, rotted to bones. It smelled awful, man, I mean enough to make you puke. Then it was just gone. Like I told you, I think I'm losing it here." He went silent for a moment, just pulling off his cigarette. Richard could hear ESPN playing in the background. "But last night, that smell was only part of it. I woke up around three…funny thing, Richard, I always wake up around three…and I'm gasping for breath again. I laid there for maybe an hour. By then I was sure I was just having a nightmare. I got up, went into the bathroom and took a piss. I didn't turn the light on. I went to the sink and I got a drink of water and…Christ almighty…there in the dark, I…I thought I saw someone fucking *standing right behind me.* A shape, a form, I just don't know. I only saw it for a second, Richard, but…but it had yellow eyes. And it stank. God, how it stank. You ever been to a county fair in August and walked through the pig barns? That's how it smelled. I swear to you, that's exactly how it smelled. I ran out of there and I turned on every light in the joint. I stayed awake until dawn. And you know what else?"

Richard swallowed. "What?"

"I'm…I'm afraid to go to sleep," he said. "I think I'm afraid of the dark. I'm shaking just thinking about it."

Richard was shaking, too.

Maitland had stuck his nose in where it didn't belong and Mrs. Crouch or *Missy Crouch* was teaching him a lesson. She was the priestess of the sow's cult and she was driving the poor guy right out of his head.

"There's one last thing, Richard. One last thing." He paused, breathing. Maybe he was listening for the approach of Missy Crouch herself. "When I had the dream that the old witch was sucking my breath away, when I came awake from it…there was a voice in my head. I could hear it. I could hear the words it spoke. It said, *'In the end, Mr. Maitland, you'll give me what I want. You won't have a choice. You'll bring what is mine and offer it freely.'* That voice…I can still hear it, Richard. I can't seem to stop hearing it."

"Mike…"

"You've got me in a real mess here, Richard," he said, his voice breaking like he was on the verge of tears. "You're my friend and I'd do anything for you…but why the fuck did you get me involved in this? Why, Richard? Why the hell did you do it?"

20

Maitland lived across town, five minutes away by car.

And that's where Richard went.

After Maitland began to sob on the phone, coming apart at the seams, he told Richard never to call him again, to stay the hell out of his life. Then he slammed the phone down. And, oh, it was bad enough that this was happening to Holly and him—an absolute atrocity, in fact—but the idea of them targeting Mike Maitland...no, that was unacceptable. He tried calling Maitland back, but all he got was a busy signal. So after wasting maybe thirty minutes doing that and another ten hemming and hawing over whether he should go over there or whether he was completely overreacting, he jumped in his car and did the right thing.

When he pulled up outside Maitland's building—a big old Victorian that had been broken up into flats—he saw that all the lights were on in his friend's window on the second floor. He could even see the flashing of the TV set.

Sucking something deep into himself, Richard went in and up the stairs.

It seemed like a long climb and maybe in his peculiar state of mind, it was. Step by step, the feeling grew in him, that sickness down in his belly that he was going to find something he was not going to like.

Outside Maitland's door, he knocked off and on for two or three minutes.

There was no answer.

Inside, he could hear ESPN's SportsCenter rambling on, something about the Minnesota Vikings first-round draft pick being out for the season with a rotator cuff injury. Other than that, he could hear nothing in there.

Well, he thought, *well.*

The door was open and he went in, that sick feeling in his belly twisting in on itself until he thought he would vomit. It settled into his guts in a heavy black mass, bunching and expanding, filling him.

Standing in the doorway, he said, "Mike? Mike? You there?"

No answer, of course.

Richard stood there, unable to go farther, feeling like some invisible hand was pressed to his chest, holding him back. But there was no hand. There was just that macabre sense of expectation, of dread discovery, the knowledge that Maitland was there. *Dead*. This is what held him back, because he did not want to see this. There were things in life you could look on and forget about and there were those other dark things that would stay with you until your dying day. And Richard knew that's what he was facing, something that would rip out his soul and piss all over it, pick open a sore in his mind that would never stop bleeding.

A voice in his head told him: *You'll find him hanging from the light fixture because what you brought into his life, what infected him, was too horrible to live with and maintain sanity. You'll find him hanging by his belt because guys like Mike Maitland always use their belts. His face will be purple and blue, his tongue hanging out like that of a dog. He'll be rotating slowly in a grim Danse Macabre semicircle, which is the last step learned by suicides who favor the noose.*

But Richard did not find him hanging.

Maybe it would have been easier if he had.

He took a step, then another, smelling something. It was like a trail leading him in, pulling him in deeper and demanding he look upon the very thing he had come to see. The smell became a stench and at first he thought maybe it was something terribly prosaic like sewage, like leaking pipes backed up with black clods of human waste.

But it was nothing like that.

What he smelled reamed out his nose, stirred his guts, and made his eyes water. It was *her*. It was the foul aroma of the swine and he knew that stink well enough by that point. The acidic smell of her shit, the acrid sharpness of her piss, the hot meat smell of her sex. It seemed to seep from the walls and ooze from the nap of the carpeting beneath his feet, drip from the ceiling and rise like steam from the furniture as if she had marked this place as a wolf might mark its lair: by pissing on everything, rubbing herself on the upholstery, squeezing out her juicy glands on the rug.

He could almost hear her voice coming out at him from the shadowy corners: *Of course I was here, you little nit. Did I not warn Maitland? Did I not send my hagwife familiars hopping and crawling in the night to dissuade his curiosity with fever-dreams and night-haunts? He was arrogant, he was proud, he would not pay heed to his own instincts. He looked to the barren sky for protection and not down at the good fertile earth, which is the mother of all, the seed and the sprout. Given no choice, I named him as I have named others and once named, he belonged to me. He was tasked with bringing to me what is mine and offering it freely. Thus I came in the night, oh yes, I came for the offering he must lay at my feet. He screamed like a violated unplowed maiden and how I made him squeal as I took him into my mouth and sucked the juice from his sweet bobbing fruit and gnawed his bollocks to pulp…*

Stumbling forward, tears filling his eyes, Richard found the blood.

It was on the floor like an explosion of red ink that stained the walls and still ran like red tears down the TV screen. This is where it happened, he knew, this is where the ritual of old was practiced at the altar of the new…where technology failed beneath the dark beckoning of an ancient pagan horror. The past overwhelmed the present and in plain view of Maitland's much-worshipped plasma TV. The disparity was mind-boggling. A smeared blood path led away to the window, which was broken out. Two stories up, she had taken her expiation, and dragged Maitland's neutered carcass out into the night, perhaps to parade his sexless, castrated form before the eyes of the primeval stars above.

Richard, boiling with hate, vowed vengeance, vowed bloody reprisals and devastating wrath against the sow for the desecration of his friend…but even then he knew the folly of it. Male blood rose high and hot when friends or lovers were misused or hurt, but it settled back into low, cool places quick enough.

The swine had destroyed his wife, his best friend, and in the end the only one who would be hurt was Richard himself and he knew it.

21

This is my wife, Richard thought when he got home in the wee hours of the morning and saw the hag waiting for him there, plotting and scheming, growing fat and repulsive as he grew thin. *This is what she has become.*

Not a woman any longer, not his lover and best friend, but a nameless thing, a great and rolling blob of white fat that had been pressed into a mold, formed into something remotely womanlike, something yeasty and warm and doughy with flashing eyes like liquid mercury.

"Well, you've come back, have you?" that scraping voice of broken sticks and choking earth said. "And how is your little playmate? The little boy who could not stop peeking and prying and asking the wrong questions?"

"You could have told me," he said in a defeated voice, "and I would have made him go away, made him forget about all this. You didn't have to...do what you did."

"What joy would there have been in that?"

Richard just stood there, smelling her corruption: brine and infection, hot and secret things that grew in damp darkness.

"Tell me of your pain, Richard. Let me suckle it."

He could not seem to breathe, to get enough air into his lungs to make his head stop spinning. His insides felt loose like an unwound spool of string. The flesh at his spine and neck tingled. His hands became fists and there was a taste of blood in his mouth.

"I want to speak to my wife," he said, trying to keep his head, trying to stop his hands from beating that leering face to blood and pulp.

"Your wife is gone, Richard," the hag said, gnashing her teeth. "She's been gone for many days now."

"You…you killed Holly?"

"Killed?" The hag cackled with a noise like shattered mirrors and screeching iron. It echoed through the room and settled into his skull where it reverberated, making him want to put a gun in his mouth and end it. "Don't be so fucking naïve, Richard. Death has little to do with it. What did you think this was all about? What did you think we wanted her for? Did you think we were only *borrowing* her and that we would return her unharmed when we were finished? Is that what you thought? Is that what you *really* thought?" She started cackling again and it was so sharp, so cutting, he had to actually press his hands over his ears. Her laughter had the tonal quality of a buzz saw. "Oh, Richard, even after all you've witnessed, you're still terribly naïve, aren't you? You believe in the triumph of good over what you consider evil. You believe in fairy-tale endings and sad faces that learn to smile. *Rubbish, sheer rubbish.* Your wifey was but a convenient incubator that I appropriated for my uses, a womb and no more. I had her and I'll have you. In the end, you'll lay with me because it is customary and freewill is no longer part and parcel of who and what you are. Yes, in the end you'll lay with me. You'll bring to me what is mine and offer it freely."

Richard screamed in rage and threw himself at the hag, but he never made it.

A searing wave of heat hit him and flattened him. He lay there on the floor, numb and senseless, choking on his own tears and nausea and helplessness. It was over. He was too late and now there wasn't a damn thing he could do to save Holly.

Not a damn thing.

He tried to rise and the hag snarled at him, rising up like a balloon, stinking and bulging, inflating until it seemed she would burst. A putrescent thing filled with corpse gas and feathered with mold. Slime exuded from her pores and black blood ran from her orifices. The only thing alive about her were those eyes…silver and purple galaxies imploding, crying tears of rank arterial blood.

"Do not interfere, Richard. The time is far past for that. The time of the birthing approaches and you will not obstruct that holy event," she warned him. "If you do, there will consequences. Your wifey can be a corpse bride at my bidding. Her heart will not beat and her lungs will not breathe. She will embrace you as a living hide…"

He began to sob and the hag only cackled.

"When you look upon me again," the beast said, "it will be because I have compelled you to give unto me what is mine by birthright."

Richard felt himself stand, felt himself walk out the door as the hag began to deflate with a hissing sound like a hot-air balloon in descent. The air was dirty and rancid with the stench of decomposition. He heard the door slam behind him and then he was walking down the stairs, finding his chair and sitting in it.

And that's where he found himself several hours later.

22

Like coming off an alcohol or drug binge, he came out of it slowly. He slept off and on until nearly noon when his bladder forced him up, forced him to take some sort of action. And even when he finally did, he could not shake that sense of *invasion,* that sense that he had been nothing but a wind-up toy to the hag upstairs. That she turned the key, made him walk from the room, made him sit in the chair. That she had completely drained his will.

The memory of it was almost too much.

If automobiles had minds, they would have felt as he did. That something had climbed inside of him and driven him. Made him go, made him stop, and he had utterly no say in the matter.

After he relieved himself, he climbed in the shower and turned on the spray. First ice-cold to revive himself, to drag him up from the cellar of his brain. And then hot, to physically wake him, chase away that numbness, that feeling of violation. He was in there nearly fifteen minutes, scalding himself, and more than once he'd had to stuff a wet washcloth into his mouth and bite down on it. Then he would scream, scream with that muffled, gurgling sound, sucking in hot water and spraying it back out. It was ridiculous, but he would not let that hag upstairs know of his pain and torment. She would not feed on his terror and nourish herself with it.

After he dressed, he went upstairs to destroy what he found.

In the end, it was all unnecessary, for she was gone.

Holly was gone.

Of course she was gone. She had been gone a long time. Missy Crouch had arranged it all. She had selected Holly by pure chance. She had defiled her and possessed her and all to make her a fertile surrogate breeding ground for the children of the sow and Old Jack Hobb.

Richard stood in the doorway, naked, still dripping from the shower. He had a hatchet in his hand that he had taken from the garage. He had come to chop the sow into kindling. And he had no earthly doubt that he would have done it, too, had she been there.

She would have gotten into your mind, stopped you.

"No," he said, very calmly. "Not this time. I would have killed her."

Maybe. But what you would have killed was Holly's body, the hag would have flown. The police would have found you with your wife's body. A drooling, delusional lunatic who chopped up his innocent pregnant wife and unborn baby. You wouldn't be able to verify any of it and you know it and when they questioned poor, tearful, spiritually broken Aunt Pauline, she would tell them that she knew something was going on because you simply were not acting right. You would have become a tabloid star: the madman who murdered his wife and child in cold blood. WHY DID HE DO IT? the headlines would say. WHAT POSSESSED HIM?

"But the SlimCam, the SlimCam…"

Who are you kidding? Do you think she'd allow the video to exist?

Pigwicken was sitting on the nightstand.

Just looking at it, he felt the nightmares blossoming in his head. They were not of his wife, those nightmares were gone now for the most part. Even the memory of Holly herself seemed dulled, misty. No, the nightmares that rolled through his mind were all of Mike Maitland. What it must have been like for him when his sane, orderly world was turned inside out and something with yellow eyes drifted out of the shadows, something that took hold of him and destroyed him on some primary level, made him see things that squeezed his mind dry. Made him want to die. Made him beg the sow to put him down in the darkness where there was no pain. And the sow had. In the traditional way.

He heard Pigwicken breathing.

"Left you behind, has she?" Richard said.

The imp stared at him. Its chest rose and fell.

It was left behind to torment you.

He didn't doubt it. With the swine gone, the familiar would come for him in the night to suckle his throat and fill itself with his blood.

He walked slowly over to it. He took it in his hands and felt the greasy fur and that oddly warm and pebbly flesh. The weight of it, the very feel of it sickened him, the sense that it was not dead, that it was still horribly alive and full of terrible potential. Its vapid black eyes looked into his own, the grinning mouth showed him its fine, sharp teeth. There was something almost hypnotic about looking at it, feeling the muffled beat of its heart like that of a baby felt through smothering blankets. He felt dopey, ungainly, like he'd been shot up with Demerol.

But it had no power over him.

Fetishes, he knew, only had power if you believed and he no longer believed in anything but justice.

He stood there, holding it in one hand, the hatchet in the other. It began to move. At first he thought it was just some crazy hallucination, but it was no hallucination. The thing was horridly alive, moving bonelessly in his grip. A worm sculpture. The feel of its musculature was hot and obscene. *You would set me down and walk away from this, Richard. You don't know what I can do, what we can do. What we did to Maitland, we can do to you. His will was much stronger than yours, yet we bent it, we molded it to our liking like warm clay. When we showed him the things that crawled in his mind, gave them flesh and form and intent, he lost his sanity. He begged us for death as you will. He lay down, offering the sow what she wanted. Offering it willingly—*

But it was too late for anything as pedestrian as scare tactics.

That slithering, grotesque little monstrosity did not even realize how late it was. But it was beginning to realize. It squirmed in Richard's hand, clawing and biting at him, snapping those needle teeth, trying to work itself lose. And it kept trying right until Richard pressed it against the floor and took its head off with the hatchet. He kept chopping and hacking it as it writhed, pissing a black, tarry blood into the carpeting. But in the end, it simply died.

Died squealing like a slit piglet.

Died knowing pain.

And Richard was happy for this.

23

The farmhouse.

It began there, so it had to end there.

It was too late for Holly and him now. Much too late. But there would be others, he felt there would be others, and he would not let anyone else suffer like this, he would not let the sow kill innocence and seed evil. The farmhouse was a nucleus for it all. Maybe terrible things had happened there long before the Elders moved in with their iniquity. Maybe the house had a history of dark events and it had attracted those two because of it.

Regardless, it was at an end now.

Richard got there in the late afternoon. He stood looking at that tormented tree for some time. Then he went out to the SUV and came back with a 12-gauge Remington pump. He kicked open the door and went in. Dust was suspended in the air like flakes of snow. There was a stink of wetness, of dissolution, of things going to bones in ditches. And the atmosphere, of course: brooding and oppressive, crawling up his spine. It was rank and riven.

He went into the parlor.

There was nothing to see. He stepped in there merely for nostalgia's sake, to remember a better time and a better place that was now lost to him. The last time he had been in there it had been with Holly and she had been pregnant and healthy, her cheeks nicely blushed and her eyes so very blue. How beautiful she had been that day before the obscenity worked its way into her.

Outside, Richard walked over to the piggery.

As he stood before the low doorway, he heard the hysterical squealing of the sow from within. She was grunting her happiness. She had called to him and he had obeyed, dragging himself here to fall prostrate at her cloven feet.

He told himself that he could run anytime he chose. That he didn't have to do this. That he could come back with gasoline and douse the place and burn it down…but he knew better. The swine's magic was too strong. She wished him here, so he was here. He could not resist her. He could not hope to. He was a doll on a string and she pulled him along.

Stooping over, he entered the piggery.

It was as before: the brick sties, the filthy hay and straw, the disused pens, the dirty dung-spattered walls, the rising stench of pig blood and pig shit. Only worse this time because it was not a memory or even a ghost-smell, but the real thing, moist and organic. It filled the long, narrow building, seeming to pupate in the air, releasing a horrendous and fetid tide of stink.

Richard found it almost impossible to go farther.

The air was hot, seething with that awful smell. It crawled right down his throat and nested in his belly, sending waves of warm nausea rolling through him as flies crawled over his face.

He found Maitland's corpse right away.

It was hanging from a hook suspended above. He should have been shocked at the sight of it, or at least at the gruesome condition of it, but he wasn't. He was beyond shock. He stopped and looked at it with a gnawing, sinking feeling inside, but there was no emotion. The hook was driven through the back of Maitland's skull and it must have taken considerable strength. But as grisly as that was, it was nothing in comparison with his remains.

The sow had been eating on him.

She had started between his legs and chewed a wedge-shaped chasm up into his abdomen, gnawing right through the pelvic girdle, it would seem. Flies lit off the corpse, rising and descending like a cloud of black soot.

"Richard, come down here," a voice said. "There's no fear now, only revelation."

Although the voice was feminine in timbre, it was not the smooth delivery of Holly or even the scraping, reedy snarl of the hag. This was a voice he did not know.

There was someone standing near the large sty at the end as if to block his progress.

"Come down here," she said.

He did. He followed the dirt run as it angled deeper into the earth, deeper into the dark pagan mysteries of the piggery itself, a place of blood offering and rebirth, violent death and primordial regeneration. It was here in days now long past that the sows would have brooded their young and raised their squealing farrow. Here, that the huge, grunting male boars were castrated by the farmer's hand before their flesh grew sour with their own glandular secretions and they grew violent as boars tended to. And here, that the swine were slaughtered for their meat, usually in a special planked enclosure where they could not move while their throats were slit and the blood was collected in bowls for soups and sausage.

The piggery was haunted by its past, practically malignant with the death and slaughter it had witnessed. He soaked up the vile atmosphere like a sponge, became saturated with it.

Waiting for him was Mrs. Crouch.

It could have been none other. She was dressed in a cranberry-red jogging suit of all things. There was no stoop to her frame, no slouch. And that was positively disturbing because her hair was white and thinning, her narrow face fissured like pine bark. She looked as if she used time and not the other way around.

"Missy Crouch," Richard said.

The old lady tittered. "That was a long time ago, son. A very long time ago. I've used up a few lives since then. The cycles come and they pass, waxing and the waning like the phases of the moon high above."

"Witch."

"Midwife," she corrected him. "*Midwife*. I call the seeding and I see that it comes to term. There is no witchery to that, my boy, no witchery to the biology of Mother Earth and her ways, which are plentiful and sacred."

There was an edgy seam of dark fanaticism to her, he saw, yet it was tempered by a casual, motherly calm that was easy and narcotic like the golden sunshine of late afternoon. And in being so, there was nothing remotely threatening about her. She was not stirring a cauldron or casting bones about. She just stood there, smiling, her teeth worn and few.

"What's done is done, Richard. Don't you see that? You think you have come here to do a hurt to me or the sow, but you are wrong. You have come because you have been compelled to return to this place as those of true faith must in the end," she said to him. "Bless the sky and praise the earth, make your offerings to she who waits."

"I'll kill you," said.

"You may well at that, but listen to me. Give me audience for a time. I am sorry for what happened to Holly and your child. I truly am…but what is done cannot be undone. There was no hate in the selection of your Holly. It was opportunity well-seized. The sow chose her as her vessel. No more and no less. It was not done out of malice but of the need for continuance. Can you understand that?" she asked him. "Some four centuries past, I sought such a vessel in Jane Penden. The sow would have regenerated herself in that foolish child to carry the seed of her joining with Jack Hobb…but it was not to be. I have chosen other vessels for her, but each time through chance, coincidence, or interference, it has not come to pass. The sow has become weary, impatient, and angry. She wishes only to bring her brood to term."

Richard shook his head. "She is evil. She is a monster. She doesn't deserve to breed."

"She was brought forth by the Mother Earth as you were. She is a primal thing from a primal age, her ways are simple: she exists to be worshipped, to be adored, to be given the expiation that is hers by birthright, and to bring forth her children. If that is her crime, then all of nature is guilty. You think she is a demon, but she is no demon. She is a child of nature, a child with voracious appetites of the flesh and sex, an entity that is unbelievably wicked when crossed…but certainly no demon. Has she not the right as a child of the Earth Mother's womb to bring forth her kind, to be fruitful and multiply?"

"At the cost of other lives?"

"We all exist at the costs of other lives."

"She's a freak. She has to be destroyed. Now step out of my way."

"But I will not. Not until you listen and hear." Smiling almost sardonically, she reached into one of the pens and brought out a fistful of yellow hay. "But first consider this, think on it," she said, holding it up and pressing it in his direction. "This is a product of Mother Earth as you and I and the sow are. This is her seed and her kin. This is ryegrass and sweet timothy, clover and oats and barley. Is it evil? Do you hate *it?* It sprouts from the womb of the Mother Earth and follows its natural rhythms as you do, as I do, as the sow has and will yet do. Do you hate it? Do you hate the farmer that slaughters cattle so that you may have meat?"

She took a step forward like she didn't really think he would use the gun. And maybe he wasn't entirely sure himself. He'd shot skeet, he'd bagged partridge, but he had never, ever raised a weapon against another human being…or, at least, at anything intelligent.

Richard nodded. "So, you think I should walk away and forget, just forget that she destroyed my wife and murdered my child? Just go on with my life?"

"It's beyond that and we both know it. You have come in offering. You have come to lay with the sow to ensure the fertility of her crops."

"You're insane."

"I am as the good earth has made me. As you are. As the sow is. We are threads of the same skein spun by the same hand and we must accept one another."

She kept talking and talking, making no distinction between what she and the swine had done—or tried to do—and what farmers did on a daily basis. She discussed the human race in purely agricultural terms, just another crop to be harvested, stock to be butchered. Mother Earth was the harrow goddess who seeded and sown and reaped and all living things were livestock to eat and be eaten, no more, no less. Slowly, slowly, she was filling his mind with webs, cocooning up his thoughts. She was hypnotizing him. Doing something. His eyelids felt heavy. His thoughts were confused. The shotgun in his hands felt heavy as a railroad tie.

"…so you see, we all suffer in varying degrees. You have known but this one life, while I have suffered through many, wanting never anything more than what was promised me and as the sow only wishes to bear her young, her fold and farrow."

Suddenly, Mrs. Crouch was only a few feet away, smiling sweetly like a maiden aunt or a favored grandmother. Richard wanted to go into her arms, to curl up in her lap, let her stroke his hair and hum ancient songs to him. The seduction was very powerful. And the only thing that really saved him were the dusty spokes of sunlight coming in…for in it, he saw she cast no shadow.

She reached out for the gun. "Let's get rid of that, shall we? Why don't you give it to me? You can do that, can't you?"

Richard grinned. "Sure, I can give it to you."

He gave it to her point blank in the belly.

24

The blast threw her backward and down. She sat right up, a smoking crater where her belly had been. She let loose with a high, keening cry, her eyes glowing like cinders in an ash pot. No blood came from her wound. She glared at Richard with a living hatred. Even the hag that possessed his wife had not looked at him with such a blistering, searing hatred of everything he was. Missy Crouch…Alizon Clove would have ripped him to shreds, gutted him, disemboweled him, and happily rolled through his remains like a dog with rotting fish.

She was not human, she was not even remotely so. Her eyes were like living fire and Richard could feel their heat on him like cutting torches. No, this was no one's maiden aunt and this was no one's kindly grandmother, this was a feral and deranged thing, a monster. It would have skinned children and sucked the blood from infants if that would have advanced its cause.

"Traitor!" she shrieked, a mist of blood breaking from her lips. *"You are a heretic! You are not of the true calling!"*

She tried to rise back up and he gave her the butt of the Remington full in the face with everything he had. Her head snapped back on its scrawny stump of neck. Teeth flew from her bleeding mouth. The skull beneath the skin made a cracking sound like thin ice. She fell back to the dirt floor, either dead or near to it.

He stepped around her, moving toward the sty at the end. He could hear the sow moving in there, rolling in her own filth and excrement, slopping in the mud, awaiting him, grunting happily, it seemed, completely unconcerned about the fate of Missy Crouch. Yes, a simple creature, but in her simplicity narcissistic and entirely selfish. The stench was unbearable. It rose from the pen in steaming rankness, blowing out at him hot and feculent.

This was the moment he had been waiting for.

He brought up the shotgun.

He knew her power, her strength, that she could make things unpleasant with her telekinesis, but he did not back down. Too much had been taken from him and in the most malevolent of ways. His Holly overtaken, broken and perverted, converted into this lolling pink obscenity. His child used as meat to spawn a generation of monsters.

The sow raised her snout from the muck like a crocodile sensing prey. A blanket of flies misted into the air as she appraised him with glittering black eyes. He saw there was no malice in those eyes, but worse there was hunger, there was lust, there was insatiable desire…and maybe even something quite like love.

"It is mine by birthright," she said. "Offer it to me freely."

That was the moment he could have had her, could have killed the bitch and wiped her foulness from the pages of history…but he hesitated. For just one shivering, confused moment, he hesitated. The sow, no doubt realizing her predicament, showed him an image of Holly, *his* Holly, grinning up at him from the mud, eyes flashing like blue moons.

He hesitated.

Then cried out as he was attacked from behind. Missy Crouch, or the thing she was, came at him with something shining and silvery in her hands. She drove it between his shoulder blades. He half turned and she slashed him across the face, across the hands and chest. The shotgun dropped as tendons were slit. Then the final act of hobbling: he was hamstrung, dropping into the dirt, no threat to anyone.

"An offering is made," the old lady said. "Wouldst thou accept it?"

The sow rose from the mud, flyspecked, pink and shining, horribly bristled. Though she stood upon rear split-hoofed trotters, she had hands that were semi-human, the fingers puffy and scaled, the nails thick, yellowed, and splintered from pawing in the dirt. It was these that she ran over her oily, porcine flesh, giving special attention to the rows of milk-fattened teats, the bulging pregnant sack of her belly. Bluebottle flies peppered it, swollen gray ticks suckered by the dozens, ranks of mites scattering as her paws came near. What was in there moved with a greasy, rolling gyration.

The sow stepped out of the mud, standing over Richard. Clods of mud and pig shit dropped free, speckling his face. He sobbed and trembled. She snarled and growled low in her throat, globs of white foam dropping from her fleshy lips. A stream of hot, noxious, and vinegary-smelling piss ran from between her heavy thighs as she emptied her bladder on the hamstrung supplicant, anointing him in the old way and making him writhe as his skin burned. Steam rose from it. Grunting and squealing, she squatted over him, bringing her meaty flanks forward so that he might smell the appalling, flyblown essence of her loins as the fruit of her womb ripened with juicy vitality.

He cried out, pushing her away with one hand, his fingers sliding over her slippery, engorged labia.

He must have lost consciousness or was put under by the swine, because when he opened his eyes again, he was naked and greased with pig slime. The blessed event had occurred. The sow's loathsome offspring, a baker's dozen, the traditional witch's coven of thirteen, were pressed up to him, suckling his bleeding wounds with hungry, puckering mouths like piglets crowded at teats. Like Pigwicken, they had taken after their father. Squamous, swollen, baboonlike and hog-snouted, they sucked at his blood, making shrill mewling sounds. Tufts of fine gray hair were still greased with placental jelly, their eyes beady like those of rats.

Though Richard felt nearly numb from head to foot, he could still feel the suction of those little mouths draining him and, worse, he could feel the snout of the sow sniffing between his legs. Squealing with delight, she seized what was between his legs with her slavering jaws, taking what was hers by birthright.

About the Author

Tim Curran is the author of the novels *Skin Medicine, Hive, Dead Sea, Resurrection, Hag Night, Skull Moon, The Devil Next Door, Doll Face, Afterburn, House of Skin,* and *Biohazard*. His short stories have been collected in *Bone Marrow Stew* and *Zombie Pulp*. His novellas include *The Underdwelling, The Corpse King, Puppet Graveyard, Worm,* and *Blackout*. His short stories have appeared in such magazines as *City Slab, Flesh&Blood, Book of Dark Wisdom,* and *Inhuman,* as well as anthologies such as *Shadows Over Main Street, Eulogies III,* and *October Dreams II*. His fiction has been translated into German, Japanese, Spanish, and Italian.

Find him on Facebook at:
https://www.facebook.com/tim.curran.77

Bibliography

Novels

Afterburn
Bad Girl in the Box
Biohazard
Blooding Night
Cannibal Corpse, m/c
Clownflesh
Dead Sea
Doll Face
Graveworm
Grim Riders
Grimweave
Hag Night
Hive

Hive 2: The Spawning
House of Skin
Long Black Coffin
Monstrosity
Nightcrawlers
Resurrection
Skin Medicine
Skull Moon
Terror Cell
The Devil Next Door

Novellas
Blackout
Corpse Rider
Deadlock
Fear Me
Headhunter
Leviathan
Puppet Graveyard
Sow
Tenebris
The Corpse King
The Underdwelling
Toxic Shadows
Worm

Collections
Alien Horrors
Bone Marrow Stew
The Brain Leeches and Other Eldritch Phenomena
Dead Sea Chronicles
Here There Be Monsters
Horrors of War
Zombie Pulp

CROSSROAD
PRESS

www.ingramcontent.com/pod-product-compliance
Lightning Source LLC
LaVergne TN
LVHW091012080826
845145LV00003B/1243

* 9 7 8 1 6 3 7 8 9 6 2 2 8 *